Disney · PIXAR

LIGHTYEAR

IZZY HAWTHORNE: DESTINY AWAITS

Design by Winnie Ho
Composition and layout by Susan Gerber

Printed in the United States of America
First Hardcover Edition, April 2022
10 9 8 7 6 5 4 3 2 1
FAC-021131-22070

Library of Congress Control Number: 2021952265
ISBN 978-1-368-07729-3

Visit disneybooks.com

Disney · PIXAR

LIGHTYEAR

IZZY HAWTHORNE: DESTINY AWAITS

Written by Bethany Baptiste

Disney PRESS
Los Angeles • New York

Prologue

I colored the last button on my Space Ranger suit's green collar so big and red that my pointy crayon turned into an itty-bitty nub. I held the finished collar out in front of me, admiring my coloring job with a satisfied smile.

The last time I tried to make a Space Ranger uniform, I couldn't fit the collar around my hair puffs without messing them up. This time it looked perfect! But the only way to find out for sure was to try it on. I carefully fit it over my head, tugging it around my hair and down onto my shoulders.

Then I slipped on white cardboard sleeves, green-and-white wrist cuffs, and homemade green boots over my sneakers.

I raced into the bathroom and hopped onto my footstool. In the mirror, I practiced my Space Ranger stance.

Fists on hips.

Chest out.

Chin up.

Feet spread apart.

Just like Grandma taught me.

"I'm Izzy Hawthorne, and nothing can scare me, because I'm a Space Ranger!" I shouted in my bravest voice.

Oh, this would cheer Grandma up for sure!

I ran through our apartment and stretched out my arms

sun, Alpha T'Kani, could be seen in the distance. Down below, Zap Patrol officers patrolled the perimeter of the base, watching for giant vines and bugs that could sneak through and grab people.

I gave Mom a salute. "Roger that!"

On my last mission, I accidentally crashed into a security guard, and her meat-bread-meat sandwich fell on the floor with a juicy splat. She reported me to Mom, my commanding officer.

Our door hissed open for me and I bumped into Dad, who was speaking to a hologram of somebody on his wrist communicator. Oops!

"Oof! Whoa!" Dad said, stumbling back. The holographic person began to glitch. "Izzy, try to be careful." He wagged his hand to stop the glitching.

"Sorry, Dad," I apologized, giving him a super-quick hug. I walked *really* fast down the corridor, careful not to bump into anyone else.

For the last few weeks, Grandma hadn't felt very well, which meant she had to go to a special hospital ward to be more comfortable. It was my mission to make her happy while she was there.

I made spaceship thruster noises and tilted my arms to the left and the right to dodge anyone in my path. In my head, I wasn't a kid running down the halls; I was a Space Ranger piloting my ship through a dangerous belt of asteroids.

One of the nurses who took care of Grandma stopped me outside her door.

He put a finger to his lips and went *shhh,* softly.

I pressed the fake button on my cardboard wrist communicator and whispered into it, "Roger that, Star Command."

Grandma had good days and not-so-good days.

On her good days, she seemed like her usual self after her morning cup of coffee—one cream, no sugar. But on her not-so-good days, she looked so tired no cup of coffee could help. On days like that, Dad said I had to be soft and quiet. And according to Grandma, the only way for a Space Ranger to be soft and quiet was to go into "stealth mode."

Pressing my suit collar's stealth mode button, I held my breath. Her door slid open for me when I crept up to it.

"I always thought we'd get to be Space Rangers again. I missed all the adventures," I heard Grandma say. She was talking to someone, but no one else was there. Were they using stealth mode, too?

"Hi, Grandma," I said, using my inside voice.

When Grandma smiled at me, the wrinkles around her eyes always smiled, too.

"Hey, sweetheart," she said tiredly. "Come here."

I climbed up to be with her, and she pointed at the hologram camera at the foot of her bed.

"I'm leaving a message for my friend Buzz," she said softly.

My eyes grew bigger than big and I gasped. "The Space Ranger?"

A long time ago, Grandma was a brave Space Ranger, and Buzz Lightyear was her partner on Star Command missions. Together they flew a spaceship called the *Turnip*, escorting scientific explorers to supercool unknown planets.

But something went wrong, and everyone got stuck here on T'Kani Prime, where the slithery vines were mean and the giant monster bugs were meaner.

Grandma smiled a little more, like she was halfway between a good day and a not-so-good one. "That's right! He's in space right now."

I looked up at the ceiling, pretending I had powerful telescope vision. In my imagination, Buzz sat inside his cockpit, piloting his ship to zoom around rainbow planets and bright stars. I heard the *bruuuummm* of his engines spitting out roaring fire. He wore a Space Ranger suit like the one behind a glass case in Grandma's office.

"This is my granddaughter, Izzy," Grandma said to the hologram camera.

I grinned at the camera and puffed out my chest to show off my homemade uniform. "I'm gonna be a Space Ranger, too!"

Grandma asked, "Just like him?"

I shook my head and threw my arms around her, giving her a hug. "Just like you."

Even though Grandma's hug felt like a gentle squeeze, it

made me feel safer than the laser shield Commander Burnside wanted to build to keep the creepy-crawly bug monsters away from us.

As I snuggled against Grandma, she kept talking to her friend Buzz.

"Goodbye, Buzz. I'm sorry I won't be there to see you finish the mission," she said tiredly, lifting her finger to the camera. "To infinity . . ."

But Buzz couldn't answer back, and that made her cry.

"It's okay, Grandma," I said, wiping away her tears. "He'll come back."

When I hugged her again, she kissed my forehead.

"Of course he will. He always sees a mission through to the end, and this mission is no diff—" Grandma paused, her face growing sadder. "Well, I suppose this mission will be different from all the others."

I pulled back from her. "How's that, Grandma?"

She touched my cheek with shaky fingers. "Because I won't be here for him this time, Izzy. But when he comes back, he'll get my message and know I still believe in him."

"Do you believe in me, too, Grandma?" I asked, hopeful.

"More than you'll ever know, Izzy," she answered, looking at my outfit. "You'd make an excellent Space Ranger."

"You really think so, Grandma?" I asked eagerly.

She nodded, smiling like it was a good day again. "It's Buzz's mission to take you all back home safely, but he can't do it by himself. He'll need help from a cadet who's a smart cookie like you."

Grandma gave my belly a light tickle and I fell over on her lap, giggling.

"Grandma," I squealed, squirming.

"I have a mission for you," she said in her serious tone. It was her commander voice.

For a very long time, Grandma was the commander on T'Kani Prime and everyone's boss, but after she got really sick, she stopped assigning missions. That made this assignment extra special.

Which made me feel extra special.

"If you truly want to be a Space Ranger, there are three rules you need to follow," she continued. "Are you ready to hear them?"

I scrambled to my knees and gave her a respectful salute. "I'm ready, Commander."

"Rule number one: Never stop believing in yourself, Izzy. Rule number two: Always believe in the best of people, even if they don't believe in themselves. Rule number three: Always be prepared for a challenge. Is that understood, cadet?" she said.

"Affirmative, Commander Grandma!" I nodded.

A proud tear rolled down her cheek.

No matter what, I would be a Space Ranger just like Grandma.

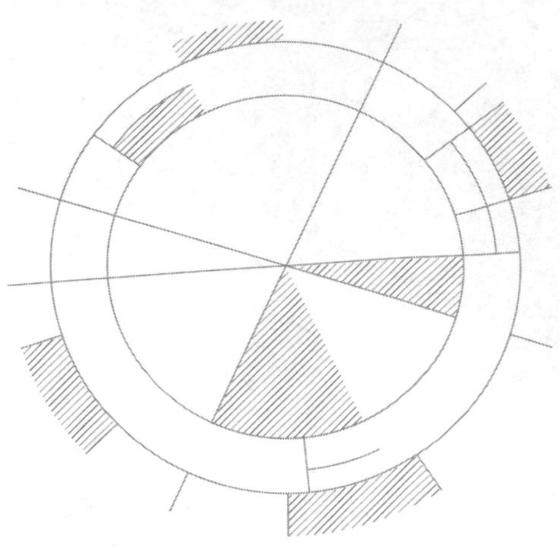

Chapter 1

Twenty-two or so years later . . .

***"It's 0700 hours. Time to wake up, Izzy Hawthorne,"* my alarm clock announced.** I lifted my head from the desk, wiping the drool off my face. Grandma's Star Command Academy rulebooks and flight manuals were scattered all over, and last night I had gone to sleep using one of them as a pillow.

"Clock, set a timer for thirty minutes." I yawned, sitting up and stretching wide.

"A timer has been set for thirty minutes," it declared.

I scurried around my apartment, getting ready. Shower, hair, teeth in the bathroom. Jumpsuit and boots in my closet. Coffee and breakfast in the kitchen.

As I ate colorful triangle-shaped morsels off my food tray, the alarm clock spoke again.

"Ten-second countdown initiating. Ten, nine, eight, seven, six," it counted down. My eyes bugged out and I shoved the rest of my breakfast into my mouth.

Ow, hot, hot, hot!

"Five, four, three, two," it continued as I raced to the door.

"One," it concluded as I skidded to a stop in the corridor, my boots squeaking loudly. *"Timer completed."*

"Mission accomplished," I said, giving myself a high five. I said good morning to everyone as I walked down the corridor and toward the elevators.

A group of us crammed into an elevator. I ended up squeezed against the back wall, but that didn't stop my good mood.

"Good morning, everyone!" I wheezed. I managed to sound bright and enthusiastic even with someone's elbow poking against my ribs.

"Morning, Izzy," everyone chorused unenthusiastically. Okay, maybe I was a little too cheery, but it was a big day. It was my once-a-month Junior Patrol training day. I loved training days.

Here on T'Kani Prime, we had a bit of a pest problem.

Actually, we had a *big* pest problem. We shared a planet with mega-sized bugs. After the *Turnip* crash-landed here and Grandma and her crew were stranded, she was faced with the challenge of keeping us safe. The bugs didn't have an appetite for humans, but they were territorial and liked to use their mandibles in not-so-friendly ways. They'd nab whoever they could, then fly above the woods and air-drop folks into trees.

So the Zap Patrol was formed to protect us, and the Junior Patrol was created to train cadets—like me—to one day join the Zap Patrol.

But for me, being on the Junior Patrol was the closest thing to being in the Star Command Academy. Studying Grandma's academy manuals helped a lot. I already knew more than most people in the Junior Patrol. But reading books wasn't enough. I knew I had to keep working hard if I wanted to live up to her legacy.

After getting off the elevator, I stopped at a framed picture of Grandma in her younger years wearing her gray commander uniform. When I was growing up, everyone said I looked exactly like her. But I didn't only want to look like her; I wanted to be a Space Ranger like her, too.

I walked outside the barracks and put my hands on my hips while surveying the planet I called home, breathing in the fresh air that smelled like mud and metal. I didn't live in a city, a town, or even a village like the ones in books I've read about Grandma's home planet. I lived on a Star Command base with a mission control center, control towers, launchpads, science labs, and a spacecraft runway.

It was built a long time ago to help everyone get home. The base was supposed to be temporary, but the mission took much longer than expected. You see, in order to get back to their home planet, the *Turnip* needed a stabilized hyperspeed crystal. With it, the *Turnip* could fly fast enough to get everyone back.

Grandma stayed here at Star Command, and her fellow Space Ranger, Buzz, blasted into space to test different hyperspeed fuel crystals, but none of them worked.

Even worse, each time Buzz returned from a

failed mission, years had passed for all of us living on T'Kani Prime, but he felt like he'd only been gone for four minutes.

It had to do with something called time dilation. Either way, Grandma got older and older waiting for him to complete his mission once and for all.

And eventually she got sicker, too.

After she died, Burnside took over as commander. According to legend, when Buzz returned from his final failed mission, he received new orders from Burnside that he didn't like. So he knocked out a few guards, rocketed a stolen ship into space, and was never heard from again.

Most believe he died somewhere up there, but a hopeful few think he escaped to another quadrant and lived out the rest of his days on a different planet.

Whether it was one or the other didn't matter. Buzz Lightyear went into outer space and never came back.

I shuddered at the thought of the endless emptiness of space.

When I was little, I looked up at the night sky. There was *so* much of it. Too much of it. I got so terrified looking at it I forgot how to breathe, and

Grandma taught me a breathing exercise to calm me down. My parents took me to a therapist, who told us I had *astrophobia*, which was a big fancy word for a fear of space.

It sounded silly to be afraid of space, but if you made one mistake up there, you'd be lost *forever.*

"Ugh, don't think about that, Izzy. No panic attacks on your favorite day of the month," I told myself, marching toward a parked rover.

Just then, a circular shadow moved across the muddy ground in front of me. A loud whiny *bzzzzzz* snapped my attention.

I'd have known that sound anywhere.

A bug had broken through the perimeter!

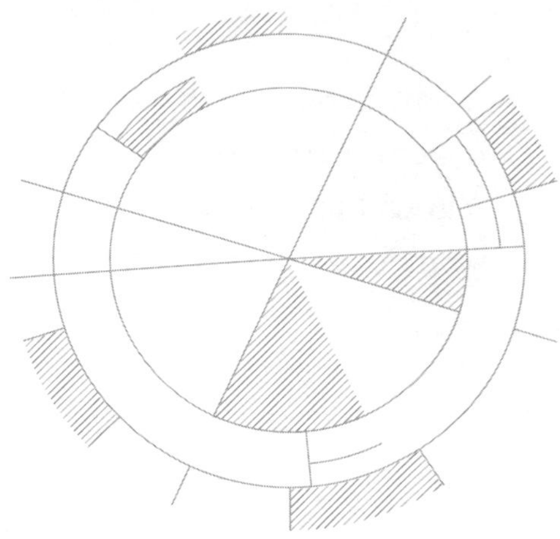

Chapter 2

"Everyone, engage in evasive maneuvers!" someone shouted from a distance. I looked up to the sky as a giant bug dove down.

Everyone in the immediate area scrambled to keep out of the bug's path.

I ran, too, mud squishing and puddles splashing under my boots. Looking up and over my shoulder, I realized the bug had selected me as its target.

"Not good, not good at all," I panted, zigzagging to confuse it.

I knew deep in my bones that if I had a blaster, I could zap it right out of the sky. I always aced my target practices. Stationary *and* moving.

But away from the training outpost, cadets weren't allowed to have blasters. Apparently it was a safety hazard. While I agreed that safety was super-duper important, I really wanted my own blaster on days like this.

Bzzzzzzzzzzzzzzz!

The bug's buzzing grew louder as it swooped down, preparing to scoop me up. As I felt the wind from its powerful wings, I heard the familiar noise of a blaster being fired. Then the bug dropped to the ground, smoke rising off it.

The Zap Patrol guard who saved me approached in full gear.

"You okay, Izzy?" she asked.

I nodded, catching my breath. "Yup. Thanks a bunch, Tonya."

"My duty," Tonya said. "Headed to the outpost?"

"You know it," I said, waving goodbye. "See you there later."

After walking back toward the truck, I waited for the rest of the Junior Patrol cadets. Soon after, a stubby gray-haired old lady with a bored, wrinkled face strolled up.

"Good morning, Darby. Are you ready for some training fun today?" I asked. Darby always arrived on time, but only because she had to. After she had gotten caught stealing a spaceship, a Star Command judge ordered her to join the Junior Patrol as a cadet. It was supposed to let her shave time off her sentence by helping out with the bug problem.

"I'm ready to fulfill my parole obligation," she deadpanned.

Giving her an encouraging smile, I said, "Whatever motivates you to be the best you can be, Darby."

"Thanks for the pep talk, kid," she said, shuffling past me to get into the rover.

"We're doing blaster target practice today," I said in a singsong voice. She smiled a little at the news and climbed into one of the back seats.

Only two things on this entire planet could make Darby smile: firing weapons that made things explode, and making things that made other things explode. She was super good at doing both. But according to the rules of her parole, Darby wasn't allowed to use any weapons without the supervision of a Zap Patrol or Star Command superior.

Our other teammate, Mo, came late as always, rubbing the sleep from his eyes.

"Sorry, I overslept." He yawned, stretching his arms high.

"It's okay," I said, giving him one of my encouraging smiles.

"No, it's not," Darby said from inside the rover.

"You still came, and that's all that matters," I continued, ignoring her.

"It won't happen again," Mo assured us as he climbed in.

Darby rolled her eyes. "It'll happen again."

Then, like always, the two began to bicker. I sighed as I climbed into the driver's seat and started the engine. Their bickering was nothing new. I had gotten used to it a *long* time ago.

To leave the base, you had to drive through colossal heavy-duty gates. Back in the day, Grandma had ordered the walls to be constructed around the base to keep the bugs at bay, but when Burnside became commander, he had started building a laser shield. Once it was ready and turned on, *nothing* would get through.

Yeah, everyone had made the best of living here on T'Kani Prime. To me it had always been home.

There were two ways to get through the forests to the Zap Patrol outpost: on foot or driving. But unless you wanted a squirmy-grabby vine to snatch you or a bug to carry you away, driving was the better option.

The long dirt road to the outpost was bumpy and muddy, which made Darby's and Mo's voices hitch as they argued all the way there. I tuned them out and hummed a happy tune as I drove.

When we arrived, I turned off the engine.

"We're here," I announced, but they kept on arguing.

"Hello," I sang, but still more arguing.

I clapped my hands together and shouted, "Hey!"

Finally, they stopped bickering and looked at me.

"We're here at the outpost to do our training," I reminded them, "which means we have to work hard as a team. Which also means no . . ."

"No arguing," Mo and Darby chorused grumpily.

We all got out of the rover. I put my hand on a scanner at the door. When the scan finished and the door slid open, the outpost was empty. We were the only ones there.

We didn't have to arrive this early. Months before, I had convinced the other two it'd be easier to come in to do our assigned chores before everyone else got there. That way we would have more time for fun stuff, like blaster target practice, paintball tag, flight practice in stimulators (well, except Darby, but we don't have time for *that* story), and firing harpoon spears.

Space Rangers didn't become heroes all on their own. That's why the corps assigned partners and teams. When you worked together as a team, you all achieved greatness.

Mo and Darby were *my* team, and we made each other better. Darby used to be a super grump, but now she was a regular grump. Mo used to make lots of mistakes. Now he only made a slightly-larger-than-average number of mistakes.

As for me, I used to only take orders. Now I'm learning to be a good leader.

I grabbed the chores tablet and read out loud what the Zap Patrol captain tasked each of us to do, but halfway down the list, the sharp sounding of a siren interrupted me.

We all looked at each other. The alarm continued to wail and wail. I had only ever heard the alarm during scheduled laser shield tests, but there was no test scheduled for that day.

Something was wrong.

All three of us ran outside, peering up as something other than a rain cloud blotted out

Alpha T'Kani, casting a dark shadow over everything. The not rain cloud was an enormous purple spaceship with a long snoutlike bow and lots of menacing cannon-guns aimed downward. It was huge.

My stomach knotted with fear.

"Uh-oh," I said, my eyes growing wide.

"Looks like we have visitors," Darby said, slightly impressed (probably by the cannon-guns), "and not the friendly kind, either."

Mo scratched his temple, confused. "Does this mean no chores today?"

IZZY AND GRANDMA'S BLAST FROM THE PAST

Zap Patrol Outpost

The rover ride to the Zap Patrol outpost was bumpy. I bounced in my seat like I was sitting on a trampoline. Grandma sat in the front passenger seat and smiled at me over her shoulder throughout the drive. The outpost was *deep* in the woods, because that's where most of the bugs lived. Grandma said she wanted to take me here because she wanted me to be prepared for when I grew up.

"A Space Ranger must map out their surroundings," she had said before our Zap Patrol escort drove us off the base. Grandma liked to drive, but her doctors said that was a bad idea, because she squinted to see faraway things and didn't like to wear glasses.

When the rover stopped, I hopped out. Grandma climbed out of the rover and held out her wrinkly hand.

"Come on, Izzy," she said to me. I took her hand and watched a Zap Patrol team jog into the woods with their blasters, ready to kick some bug butts.

"Hup, hup, hup," they chanted.

"Whoa," I said, amazed.

There were also people stationed on the outpost's walls, keeping watch with binoculars. It all looked so official.

I had never seen a bug up close before, but I learned a lot about them in school. One time, Mr. Cloud (my teacher) showed the class a hologram of one. It flew around our classroom, and some of my classmates got so scared that they ducked under their desks. I didn't, though, because I knew it was fake. But the bugs out here in the forests were real, wherever they were, and it was the Zap Patrol's job to protect us.

So I, Izzy Hawthorne, didn't need to be afraid.

"The Zap Patrol are very good at what they do." Grandma laughed, leading me toward the outpost.

IZZY AND GRANDMA'S BLAST FROM THE PAST

They sure were! Being a Zap Patrol looked almost as cool as being a Space Ranger!

"Who are they, Grandma?" I asked, pointing to people firing paintball guns at circle targets.

"That is the Junior Patrol, sweetheart," she said. "They're the cadets who have to train and learn before they can be Zap Patrol. No matter what job you do, everyone starts out as a cadet."

"You were a cadet, too, Grandma?" I asked.

She stopped walking and smiled at me. "Of course."

"Did you like it?" I asked.

"I loved it, Izzy," she answered, "but I love the jobs I do now, too."

I looked up at her, confused. "Grandma, I thought your only job was being the commander."

She nodded and bent down to my level. "Being a commander is one of my jobs, but being a wife, a mother, and a grandmother are important jobs to me, too."

What she said made my heart grow big, and I threw my arms around her, hugging her tight.

She hugged me back, then pulled away. "All right, what's our objective?"

"Every Space Ranger must map out their surroundings," I said, repeating what she told me earlier.

She smiled at me again. "Very good."

Grandma stood up, but she grimaced like her bones hurt.

"Commander, are you all right?" the rover driver asked.

"I'm fine, I'm fine," she promised.

As we walked, everyone stopped what they were doing and saluted Grandma. After we got inside the outpost, my jaw dropped at how busy it was. There was a line at the vending machine for sandwiches and tables for eating. There were rows of bunkbeds for sleeping. There was talking, laughing, and some snoring, too.

Outside in the quad, there were crates

stacked high, weapon racks on the wall, and even an old ship! Some of the Zap Patrol were loading crates into the ship.

I had never seen a ship up this close before. At home, I had toy models of all kinds of ships. Dad had video games where you could build your own and name it anything you wanted. When I played last night, I named one *Battlestar* and equipped it with a hundred laser-cannons!

"Grandma, what kind of ship is that?" I asked.

"It's called an Armadillo, sweetheart," she answered.

I squinted at the ship. I'd seen pictures of armadillos in school, but they didn't look like that.

Grandma noticed my confused face and laughed, pointing to its cockpit. "That part is shaped like an armadillo's head."

"Oh," I said.

When the Armadillo was all packed up, we stood far away as the ship's engines fired up. Hot air blasted our faces as it lifted off the ground and flew over the outpost walls.

"Where is it going, Grandma?" I asked, amazed.

"To the storage depot," she said. "That's where we keep extra supplies, equipment, and ships safe until we need them."

I jumped up and down, begging, "Can we ride in the Armadillo, please, please, please?"

Grandma laughed again, patting my head. "Soon, Izzy, soon. Before that, I want to take you somewhere very special."

I skipped behind her as she took me back inside. We went down a hallway and ended up in a room with patrol suits hanging in open lockers.

"Grandma," I gasped, looking around, "this is so cool."

"This is the gear-up room, Izzy," Grandma said. "This is where the Zap Patrol get ready for their missions."

IZZY AND GRANDMA'S BLAST FROM THE PAST

I walked up to one of the suits. Like the rest, it had mismatched parts. The metal arms and legs were all different colors, and some parts looked very old. They were like pieces of different puzzles that somehow fit together to make something entirely new.

"Grandma, why do they look like this?" I asked.

"Just because some parts are old doesn't mean they aren't useful, Izzy," Grandma said, walking up behind me. "Every piece has an important purpose. In the same way, every person here, cadet or not, has an important purpose—like you have an important purpose, Izzy."

I turned around to face her, shocked. "I do?"

"Of course you do, Izzy," she said, putting her hands on my shoulders.

"What's my purpose, Grandma?" I asked.

"Only you can find that out by listening to your heart," she said, gently poking my chest.

I squeezed my eyes tight and tried to listen to my heart, but I didn't hear anything.

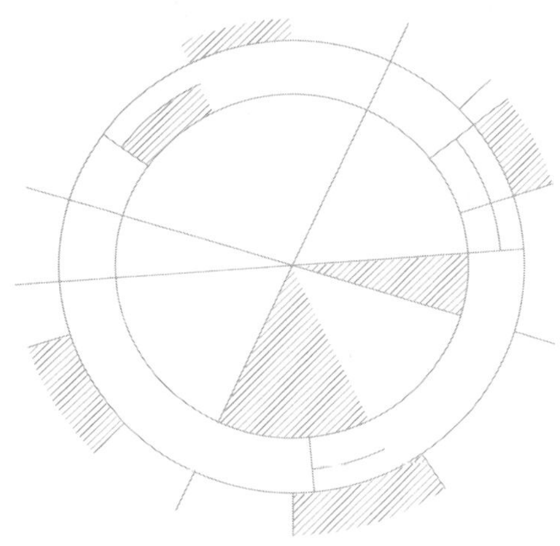

Chapter 3

I pressed the play button on my wrist communicator so we could watch Commander Burnside's final transmission for the hundredth time. The hologram version of him shouted at everyone to get into the base, quickly, as robots fired in the distance.

It had been one week since the big purple alien spaceship arrived over T'Kani Prime. The ship sent down an army of one-eyed yellow robots that Mo named zyclopes (because *zyclops* sounded cooler than *cyclops*).

That was when Burnside activated the laser shield to protect everyone.

Well, except us.

I frowned. “My heart isn’t in a talking mood today.”

Grandma tossed her head back and laughed. Then she cupped my cheek and said, “Oh, don’t worry, Izzy. There’ll come a day it’ll talk to you. It only happens when you need it the most. Trust me.”

We got locked out, but the outpost was the perfect hiding place.

Even though most of the zyclopes were still firing at Burnside's laser shield, some stomped around the woods farther from the base. It was like they were looking for something, but we didn't know what. None had discovered us, but from my scouting missions, I was able to learn two things:

1. They were controlled by the Zurg ship. They came down together and went up together. And on the ground, they moved together, like ants, following directions sent from above.
2. They used these disk thingies on their chests to teleport back to the ship.

When Commander Burnside's message finished, I went over to the projector and turned it on. Mo had programmed it to spit out mini hologram versions of the base underneath the laser shield with the robots surrounding it and the Zurg ship hovering above it.

"All right, team. Gather round. We need a plan to deal with—um—that," I said, pointing to the Zurg ship.

Up until the Zurg ship and its robots invaded T'Kani Prime, I was just a leader in training. Sure, I was in charge of our little team of three, but that was just for practice. Now the rest of the Zap Patrol was stuck behind Burnside's shield, and we were on our own.

Mo and Darby looked to me for direction, and I couldn't let them down. And I couldn't let Grandma down, either, because she taught me everything it took to be a leader.

"We need to figure out our first step," I said.

"Kill the robots," Darby said, pointing to the hologram robots.

"But to kill the robots, we have to destroy the ship," I said, pointing to the hologram Zurg ship. "So we'll fly up there, blow up the ship, and then SURPRISE, ROBOTS!"

"Like a surprise party?" Mo asked.

I smiled. "Yeah, like a surprise party. They won't know what hit them. Hey, we should totally call our plan Operation Surprise Party. All in favor say aye!"

"Aye," Darby said.

"I like the name Operation Puppet Master," Mo suggested, using his fingers to cut invisible strings.

"Because the Zurg ship controls the robots like puppets, and we're gonna cut the strings."

"You should've thrown your idea in the ring earlier," Darby said, shrugging.

I put my hands on my hips, feeling proud of us. We'd come up with a good plan and given our plan a good name, too!

"Operation Surprise Party is on!" I said excitedly, holding a fist in the air.

Then Mo scratched his head, asking, "Um, how are we gonna fly up there?"

"We'll have to use the Armadillo," I said, pointing to the nearby tall, burly gray ship with egg-yolk yellow features and the windshield of a cockpit for its face.

"Who's gonna pilot it?" Mo asked.

"Darby," I answered. If she could steal a spaceship, then she had the skills to pilot the Armadillo.

But Darby held up her palms and shook her head. "Oh, no. First off, I'm not allowed to operate anything with an engine. *Especially* not a ship. Be a violation of my parole. Second, I don't know how to fly a ship. If I was any good at it, I wouldn't have crashed one, got caught, and got put on—*you know*—parole."

Before the alien invasion, I had begun to take Armadillo piloting lessons, but it was mostly studying the manuals, talking about safety, and taking long tests about the cockpit's control panel buttons and switches. I couldn't actually *fly*.

Maybe Mo was secretly a master at piloting. I looked at him hopefully.

"Sorry to burst your balloon, but I have no idea how to fly that thing," Mo said.

My excitement for Operation Surprise Party deflated like a birthday balloon letting out squeaky air. I tried not to show my disappointment, because Hawthornes didn't stick their bottom lips out and pout. Hawthornes kept their chins up and stayed confident and brave even in the scariest of times. That's what Grandma would do.

"Okay, so we need a pilot," I said, looking up at the sky like one would fall from it. Yeah, right. But there had to be another way to get up to that Zurg ship.

I concluded our team meeting and turned off the hologram projector.

"Where are you going?" Darby asked as I walked away.

"To do a scouting mission," I answered.

And think, I wanted to say but didn't. I didn't want to show Mo and Darby that I wasn't confident in our plan just minutes after making it.

Even though there were laser-firing robots roaming about, scouting helped me think. Leaving the outpost, I went into the woods. Colossal trees stretched and stretched to the sky. Mud squished under my boots. The air was hot and sticky like always. I pushed through damp underbrush and walked around large boulders. I found no robots around, which meant the Zap Patrol outpost was safe for a little longer.

Then, suddenly, a vine snaked around my leg. When it yanked at me, I stumbled against a tree and hugged it tight. The persistent vine tugged harder and harder, lifting my feet off the ground.

I gritted my teeth and growled as it won the tug-o-war and I lost my grip. As my butt slid across the dirt, I grabbed a fallen branch and hit it.

"Leave!"

THWACK!

"Me!"

THWACK!

"Alone!"

THWACK!

After the final smack, it let go and fled underground. Tossing the branch aside, I stood back up, panting. I climbed onto a low boulder to catch my breath. Staring up at the sky, I narrowed my eyes at the Zurg ship.

Grandma's rule #3 was to always be prepared for a challenge, but I couldn't figure out how to get up there without a pilot. If only things fell out of the sky when you needed them most.

Something streaked across the sky. I scrunched my face, trying to see what it was. It was too small to be a comet or an asteroid.

"Is that a . . . ship?" I muttered.

My mouth dropped open as a space jet nosedived from the clouds. I could tell it wasn't another "gift" from the Zurg ship, because the zyclopes always arrived in pods. No, this was different. This ship was falling, and falling fast!

I slid off the boulder and raced in the direction I'd seen it go.

The muddy ground helped me skid to a stop behind the chunky tree trunk. I peeked around it as the ship landed roughly. I scrunched my eyebrows at the ship's build. It had a sharp, pointy nose and a yellow glass canopy over the cockpit, with downward-sloped wings. It reminded me of the XL toy ships my dad had 3D-printed for me when I was little.

The cockpit's canopy popped open and the pilot fired a flare gun.

"No, no, no!" I whispered, shaking my head. If the robots hadn't detected the crash landing, they'd totally see the bright flare shooting high in the air. It was like yelling out, *HEY, ROBOTS! I'M HERE TO BE ROASTED BY YOUR LASERS!*

Accompanied by an orange robot cat, the pilot climbed down and removed a canister from his ship's fuel panel. Inside it, something glowed bright, like a power source of some sort.

But before I could get a better look, I heard something:

A robot.

Its footsteps got louder and louder.

As the pilot scanned his surroundings, oblivious to the incoming danger, I knew I had to do something.

So I ran.

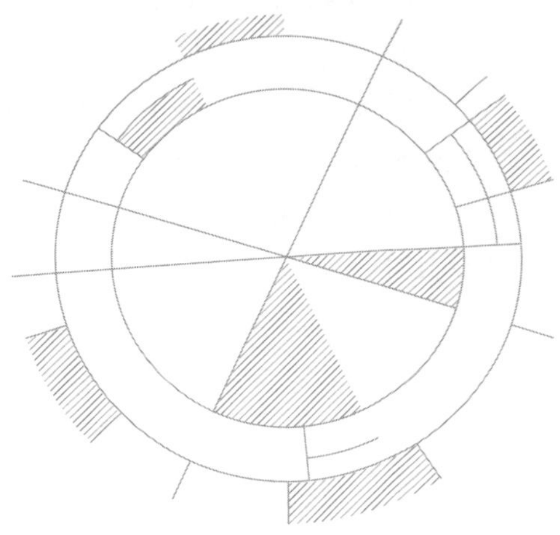

Chapter 4

My boots thumped hard and fast on the muddy ground as I charged at the pilot. When he turned around, I tackled him behind a giant boulder.

"Hey, hey!" he yelled, struggling against me.

In a panic, I pushed his face into the mud to keep him quiet.

"*Shh!* The robots!" I warned in a loud whisper, continuing to hold him down with my hand.

He growled out, "The *what*?"

I clenched my teeth, whispering, "The *robots*!"

His cat sat silently beside us, watching as we whisper-bickered with each other.

A heavy *thud-thud-thud* filled the air, interrupting our argument. We watched a zyclops exit the woods and stomp over to the pilot's crashed ship.

A zyclops was twice the height of a human and super bulky. Each had a neckless dome-shaped head, a single glowing red eye, three-clawed hands, and laser-blaster palms. Most of their bodies were yellow, and their joints were cloudy gray. Their heavy feet shook the ground with every stomp.

A zyclops's body was a weapon from head to toe.

The last thing you wanted was the attention of one.

But if the pilot didn't stay quiet, our hiding spot would be found out.

"What? Hey, that's my ship," the pilot mumbled in disbelief.

He obviously wasn't listening.

I pressed his head down a little more to try to keep him quiet.

"Wait, what's it doing?" he whispered, panicked and confused as the robot's glowing red eye scanned across the ship.

I hushed him, afraid all his talking would give

away our hiding place. If I had to play a game of hide-and-seek, I didn't want it to be with a towering monster made of metal!

I squinted as the robot took one of the weird metallic disks off its chest and stuck it onto the spaceship. The robot tapped the disk, and in the blink of an eye, it and the ship disappeared.

"Hey! No!" the pilot shouted, shooting to his feet in a panic.

I fell back on my butt and stared up at him sternly, whispering, "Be quiet!"

His cat was the only one who knew how to follow directions in life-or-death situations! Even though the zyclops was gone, that didn't mean there weren't more of them waiting to capture us in their three-clawed grips.

The pilot swiveled to me. "Where'd it go?"

Staying low behind the boulder, I pointed at the gigantic spacecraft looming evilly, like a predator ready to gobble up the entire planet.

"Up there," I said.

The pilot gaped at the Zurg ship. "What is that? What is going on?"

"Get down!" I whispered fiercely, grabbing his arm. I gave it a good strong yank to bring him back behind the boulder with me. My attention then snapped up to the Zurg ship as it spat out an angular zyclops transport pod. My stomach churned with fear.

"Shoot. Come on!" I said urgently, getting up and sneaking away.

He and his robot cat followed closely behind as I moved stealthily up a hill and toward some trees perfect for using as cover. As we crept along, my head wagged back and forth, surveying our surroundings. I kept my ears keen for the *thump-thump-thump* of zyclops footsteps, but I heard nothing: a telltale sign we were safe.

For now.

"They must have seen your ship land, too," I said.

"Who?" he snapped.

Again, I jabbed an accusatory finger at the alien ship above. "The robots!"

"Why are there robots? Where did the robots come from?" he demanded, throwing his hands up. I thought about all his questions since I tackled him—I mean, since I *met* him and his quiet observant cat. He sure did have a lot of questions when he was the one who'd fallen out of the sky.

I scanned him all the way from his smudged glass helmet to his gray boots, the same way the zyclops had scanned his ship.

The Zap Patrol suit I wore was a mismatch of old, recycled outfit parts I'd had to make fit me. But his flight suit looked like it had been designed for him and only him to wear. It was shiny and new, like nothing I had seen before. He held a rectangular canister with a glowing spiky crystal inside.

He didn't look like he belonged on T'Kani Prime.

Actually, he looked like he didn't want to be on T'Kani Prime, either.

"Where did *you* come from?" I asked, turning to keep going forward.

"I came from here!" he said, pointing to the ground.

"Here?" I blinked, confused.

My feet stopped walking and I turned around.

The Star Command launchpad hadn't been used in twenty-two years. Not since . . .

As he wiped the mud from his face, I realized that face was very, very familiar.

"Wait," I said, reaching out to wipe mud off the pilot's nameplate. My eyes widened as I read his last name not once, not twice, but three times.

I gasped, "Buzz?"

Buzz looked at my HAWTHORNE nameplate as I removed my helmet to make sure he wasn't a figment of my imagination. At my apartment, I had a framed picture of him and Grandma during their younger days at the Academy—a picture Grandma had told me to keep safe.

Buzz, stunned and maybe a little scared, stared at me like I was a ghost. "Alisha? But . . . but how?"

An ache hit my heart like a laser beam when I realized who he thought I was. It made me miss Grandma even more than I normally did. I wished she were there to see her best friend was back and safe on T'Kani Prime.

I shook my head. "Oh, no. That's my grandma. I'm Izzy."

"Izzy?" he repeated in disbelief.

I nodded slowly.

"But—but you were just a little . . ." He trailed off, holding out his hand to indicate Little Izzy height. My smile grew as I realized he must have seen Grandma's last message to him—before he defied Commander Burnside's orders, broke into the Star Command hangar, subdued a few security guards, stole a spaceship, and rocketed into space.

Buzz went pale. After a quiet moment, he looked elsewhere as something dawned on him.

Then he issued a question to his robot cat: "Sox, how long were we gone?"

A string of meows poured out of Sox, and his fuzzy ears spun as he computed an answer. Then, speaking for the first time, he announced, "Twenty-two years, nineteen weeks, and four days."

Huh, a robot cat that talked. The day was getting weirder and weirder—which was saying something, considering the Zurg ship hovering above us.

"Whoa," Buzz said, attempting to process the news.

Logic pushed aside my giddiness at seeing Grandma's longtime friend. I hadn't been Little Izzy for a very long time, but even after twenty-two years, nineteen weeks, and four days, Buzz Lightyear hadn't aged at all.

How was that even possible? Was time dilation *that* powerful?

Suddenly, my senses were on high alert as I thought I heard heavy zyclops footsteps coming toward us. I waved for Buzz and Sox to follow me into a small nearby pit. I leapt down and they followed quietly behind me. As the three of us stood there, I glanced around cautiously and listened carefully.

"I thought I heard one," I said, relieved.

"A robot?" Buzz asked.

"Yeah," I said with a nod. I was really good at listening for robots. Darby claimed it was because I had young ears.

"Wow," Buzz said, impressed.

"Well," I said, pointing at my nameplate, "I'm a Hawthorne."

Buzz propped his hands on his hips and studied the green surroundings. "You sure are. You know, your grandma and I could practically finish each other's sentences. If you're anything like her, you and I are going to make—"

"Some robots cry," I interrupted just as Buzz said "a great team." Oops. So we weren't quite ready to finish each other's sentences. But I was confident we would get there.

"A great team at making some robots cry," I amended with a grin.

He nodded warily and pointed to the ominous Zurg ship lurking overhead. "So, get me up to speed on this."

"Right. The Zurg ship showed up about a week ago."

"What's a Zurg?"

"Oh, that's the only thing the robots say, so

that's what we call the big ship. So the Zurg ship showed up, the robots surrounded the base, and then, well . . ." I paused, tapping my wrist communicator to activate Commander Burnside's hologram message.

"Citizens of T'Kani Prime: robot aliens have attacked!" he shouted as robots wreaked havoc on our home behind him. No matter how many times I watched it, I felt sad and angry seeing my fellow citizens running, surrounded by flying laser beams and fires. So much fear and destruction, and there was nothing I could do about it. Not yet, anyway.

"Everyone, get inside the perimeter! Look out!" an urgent Burnside commanded, pivoting to fire his own blaster at a zyclops. *"We're activating the laser shield immediately!"*

When the message cut off, my worry stayed put.

I said, "And that's the last we heard."

I handed my binoculars to Buzz and pointed far beyond the cave and the woods to the colossal laser dome encasing the base. As he peered into them, I could imagine what he was seeing: zyclopes firing endlessly at the impenetrable shield, as they had been for the last seven days.

"Everyone's trapped in there. No communication in or out," I explained.

Buzz fell silent, his face contemplative.

Then he looked down at his robotic cat companion. "Sox?"

The cat's ears spun and spun as he meowed.

"She's right," Sox confirmed. "No communication in or out."

"Did you just check me against your cat?" I asked, astonished that Buzz hadn't believed me at first.

"He's not a standard-issue feline," Buzz informed me. "Actually, Sox was a gift from your grandmother."

Of course Grandma would have given him a personal companion robot to help him cope after every mission. She was always thinking of ways to make life better for the people around her. Up there in space, only minutes went by for Buzz. But down here on T'Kani Prime, years went by and his friends aged.

In a way, Sox was the only thing Buzz had left of Grandma.

Sox looked up at me with his friendly green eyes and said, "Hello, Izzy."

"Hello, Sox," I said, bending down to pet him. He might have been robotic, but his synthetic orange fur was super soft!

He purred, and the vibrations tickled my palm.

Buzz frowned at the sound. "Hey, what's that noise? Don't break my cat."

"He's purring. He likes it," I said, holding back a laugh.

"Sox, *do* you like that?" Buzz asked, uncertain.

"I do," Sox assured him, continuing to purr.

"Huh," Buzz said, having learned something new about a robotic cat he'd had for years.

"Well, I hope you're ready for action. Because all we needed was a pilot," I said, nodding at him.

"For what?" he asked.

I mustered up an air of confidence, cocking my chin up. "I have a plan, and I have a team."

And the sooner I took him back to the outpost to meet Mo and Darby, the sooner we could start Operation Surprise Party.

At the mention of a plan, he gave me an impressed smile.

Yes, this was going to work.

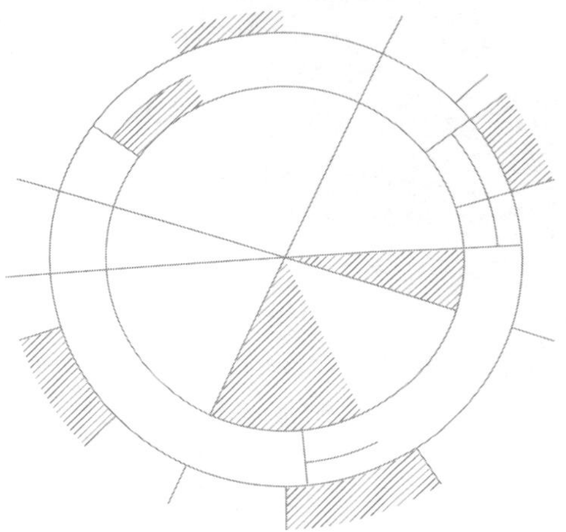

Chapter 5

Eventually, Buzz, Sox, and I reached the Zap Patrol outpost. I snuck up to the door and used the hand scanner to unlock it, and we all entered quickly.

"All right, team! Fall in!" I called out.

Mo and Darby ran out to us, fully suited up with their helmets on.

"Hup hup!" Darby and Mo chorused.

"Whoa," Buzz said, impressed.

"I found a pilot!" I announced. Then I pointed to the Armadillo parked in the fort's training yard. "Operation Surprise Party is a go!"

Buzz studied me and the team. "I like this. An elite squad. The best of the best."

He thought we were *an elite squad*? I wanted to correct him, but I had a gut feeling if I told him we were actually Junior Patrol, he'd decline his invitation to Operation Surprise Party.

With Buzz on our side, our plan would definitely work, so it didn't matter if we were a bunch of cadets. I'd memorized Grandma's Space Ranger manuals. I'd trained for this my whole life. I was fully prepared to prove that underneath my mismatched Zap Patrol suit, I was Space Ranger material.

Buzz focused on Mo and Darby, saying, "You know, her grandmother was the greatest Space Ranger in the history of the corps. It'll be an honor to work with you."

When he mentioned Grandma, a warm gooeyness tangled around my heart. Everything I did, I did to prove I was worthy of the Hawthorne name.

"You're a Space Ranger?" Darby asked.

Buzz stood up straight, tall, and proud at her question. "Affirmative."

I held back a laugh as he quickly fixed the wedgie he'd given himself by standing up *too* straight.

"I thought Space Rangers had those cool suits with all the buttons," Mo said.

"This is just temporary," Buzz said, glancing down at his space suit.

"Come on! Gather round, team!" I instructed, gesturing at them to follow me.

We huddled around the hologram projector, which showed the laser-shielded base, the attacking robots, and the Zurg ship lurking above like a menacing cloud of gloom and doom. The whole setup looked pretty official, if you asked me. Next I looked at my team to explain our even more official Operation Surprise Party.

"Let's review our objectives," I said.

"Kill the robots," Darby said, just like earlier.

"And don't die," Mo added.

I sighed. That was *not* one of the objectives we had talked about.

Darby's dour face became even dourer. "'Don't die' is just something you want to do every day."

Mo shrugged. "It's still an objective."

"Guys, guys!" I interrupted.

"If I may," Buzz interjected, "we have *one* objective."

He picked up his canister with the spiky crystal, and it glowed against the dark damp of the depot interior.

Buzz continued, "We need to put this crystal in the *Turnip* and get out of here. That's been my mission ever since I—"

He stopped himself, then said instead, "Well, since before you were born."

He trained a finger on the hologram image of the *Turnip*, adding, "So, to do that, we have to get onto the base."

"To do that, we have to kill all the robots," Darby reiterated, pointing to the hologram robots.

"To do that, we have to destroy the alien ship," I said, pointing to its holographic version.

"And to do any of that, we have to not die," Mo added.

Darby shot him an annoyed look. I turned to Buzz, determined to get this mission overview back on track.

"So, Operation Surprise Party," I said. "It's a variation on Operation Thunderspear. Didn't you get a medal for that one?"

"Well, it was two, actually," he said, correcting me, before pausing. "Wait, how do you know about Operation Thunderspear?"

My chest swelled with pride. I knew things. In

fact, I knew a whole lot about Space Ranger missions.

"I've read all my grandma's Space Ranger books from cover to cover. Twice," I explained.

Buzz nodded, looking impressed. I nodded back, pointing at my nameplate to remind him whose granddaughter I was, and turned back to the hologram.

"We've figured out the alien ship powers the robots on the ground," I explained to him. The hologram Zurg ship sent wiggly energy waves down to the robots.

"So we fly up there, we blow up the ship, and 'Surprise, robots!' "

On cue, the hologram Zurg ship blew up and the robots fell over like lifeless toys.

"You're toast," I said, watching the hologram. I went on, "Then we put your crystal in the *Turnip*—"

"And finish the mission," Buzz said approvingly.

"It's a good plan," we both said at the same time.

Then he held out his finger to me. "To infinity . . ."

The gesture looked familiar, but I couldn't remember where I had seen it before. Unless—

"Are you trying to get me to pull your finger?" I asked, crinkling my nose.

"Don't fall for it," Mo warned.

"No, not like that. It was . . . It's a thing your grandma and I used to do," Buzz admitted.

I shot a disgusted look at Mo and Darby.

Darby scrunched up her face like she'd taken a whiff of garbage. "Ew."

"I . . . We would never . . . She didn't mean to . . ." He tried to explain, looking embarrassed. Then he stopped himself and said, "Anyway, forget it. Moving on."

He walked to the dusty but trusty Armadillo, looking over the nearby stock of weapons, ammunitions, and equipment. "Let's load these munitions onto the Armadillo and steel ourselves for combat."

My heart raced in excitement and I thrust a celebratory fist into the air. "Operation Surprise Party is on!"

Sox's ears spun around and around. "Buzz, do you hear that?"

We all stopped and listened. The sound was faint, probably easier to pick up if you had robot cat ears.

"I hear something," Buzz said, nodding once. "You think it's a robot?"

"No, we've never seen a robot this far from the base," Mo said.

Erring on the side of caution, I cocked my head, listening carefully.

"I don't hear anything," I said.

CRASH!

Darby, Mo, and I leapt back in shock as a robot's arm burst through the fort's stone wall and yanked Buzz right through the gaping hole it had made.

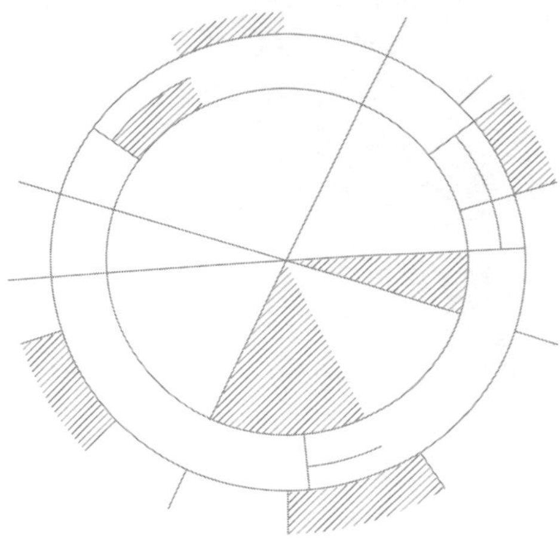

Chapter 6

I hadn't heard the robot a few seconds before, but—

"Now I do!" I shouted out at Buzz as the robot threw him back through the hole, making him drop his blaster. But when he reached for it, the robot grabbed him again.

Sox, Mo, and I rushed over to the gigantic hole in the wall, watching an upside-down Buzz try to get free from the robot's three-clawed grip. With its other hand, the bot reached for the teleportation disk stuck to its chest.

But all of Buzz's kicking knocked the disk away. The robot stomped over to it.

If the robot got to that teleportation disk,

it would take Buzz back to its Zurg ship, and I couldn't let that happen!

"Don't worry! We've got you!" I yelled, snatching up a cannon-gun. Sox meowed loudly, jumping out of my way as I swiftly loaded the cannon with ammunition I found in a crate at my feet. Heaving it onto my shoulder, I took aim and fired at the robot. A gigantic paintball exploded against its head.

The bot swiveled to stare me down. A dangling Buzz yelled as he was whipped around.

I gaped. "What?"

I looked at the crate and the TRAINING AMMO label my eyes had somehow skipped over.

Nice job, Izzy.

Real *nice*.

"Ugh," I groaned.

Though my mistake called for a good ole facepalm, there was no time for that. I glanced at another munitions crate, heartened by the LIVE AMMO stamp on it. Firing another paintball as a diversion, I walked backward to try to get some. The training ammo I fired smashed hard into the robot's shoulder plate and knocked it loose, exposing plugs and sparking wires.

Not bad, Izzy Hawthorne. Not bad at all.

"Fear not!" I exclaimed with conviction. "The Junior Patrol has your back!"

Buzz stopped struggling and yelled, "The Junior *what*?"

The robot reached out and shot an unfriendly blaster ray at me.

I barely ducked out of the way, feeling the flying beam's heat as it passed me by and hit the Armadillo instead. *Oh, no!* An explosion rattled the fort, and our ticket to the Zurg ship went up in flames.

"No! The ship!" Buzz roared, struggling to reach his captor. The robot tried again to get to the teleportation disk, but Sox flew into its face with a determined meow, using his claws to scratch at its single bright red eye.

Mo scrambled up onto the outpost's wall. He hefted a harpoon onto his shoulder and shot at the robot just as Sox's frontal attack made it stumble backward into a tree. The spear sailed dangerously close to Buzz's head and lodged in a tree trunk instead.

"Did I get it?" Mo shouted.

"Pretty close!" I said proudly, because practice makes perfect.

Mo took off his helmet. "Sorry, I haven't trained with this weapon. Let me reload."

"Not trained? What do you mean you're not trained?" Buzz yelled.

The robot knocked Sox off its face, but the cat clawed his way down the robot, causing more damage to its shoulder. Sparks flew from the exposed wires. With a slumped arm still holding Buzz, the robot began to stomp to its disk once again.

I tried shooting another diversion shot, but my cannon-gun was out of training ammo, and the nearest LIVE AMMO crate was still halfway across the quad. *Great, just great.*

"You there! Grab it! Grab it!" Buzz shouted frantically at Darby, pointing to the blaster lying at her feet.

"Grab what?" Darby asked, looking at the ground in confusion. Like Mo, she was struggling to see with her helmet. When she took it off, she saw the blaster and held up both of her hands in surrender.

"Oh. No. I'm not allowed to handle weapons. Be a violation of my parole."

"Parole?" Buzz exclaimed.

Since Darby and the blaster were much closer than the LIVE AMMO crate, I took matters into my own hands and discarded my cannon-gun.

I raced to the blaster and scooped it up. "Buzz!"

"Izzy, now!" he ordered.

I chucked the blaster hard just as Buzz reached out his hand . . . but it was the wrong hand.

"Huh?" he yelled, confused until he noticed it sailing past on his other side. "No!"

"Okay, new plan!" I called back, trying to think one up.

"New plan?! What was the old plan?" Buzz shouted, exasperated. He used all his strength to lift himself right side up and pull at one of the two remaining fastener bolts on the robot's dangling arm. It slumped even more, sending Buzz upside down again.

The robot extended its other hand to the transportation disk, but another one of Mo's harpoon spears got there first.

Then the disk and the spear blinked out of sight.

The Zurg ship would definitely be in for a surprise when that arrived!

"Did I get it?" Mo asked from above.

"A little to the left!" I shouted back.

While the robot aimed at Mo in revenge, Mo was too busy reloading his harpoon to even notice he was seconds away from becoming the zyclops's target practice.

I opened my mouth to yell at him to move, but Buzz yanked out the robot's last shoulder bolt, throwing its aim off. Mo yelped, nearly falling off the wall as the laser beam almost hit him.

Buzz fell to the ground, and the severed robot arm fell, too.

It malfunctioned, sending out random blasts.

One of them flew at me, and I dodged it quickly.

Phew! That was a close one!

Using its remaining attached arm, the robot grabbed Buzz's ankle. Buzz pulled the severed arm close and tried to aim at the robot's head, but the arm fizzled out and died.

Mo shot another spear, and it hit the smoldering robot's neck!

The robot sputtered and sparked. The ground shook as it dropped to its knees with a loud thud.

"Did I get it?" Mo shouted.

I smiled proudly and gave him a thumbs-up. "You got it!" I shouted back.

Mo pumped a celebratory fist into the air. *"Yes!"*

The zyclops fell over, dropping Buzz. But Buzz didn't look happy.

In fact, he looked super annoyed.

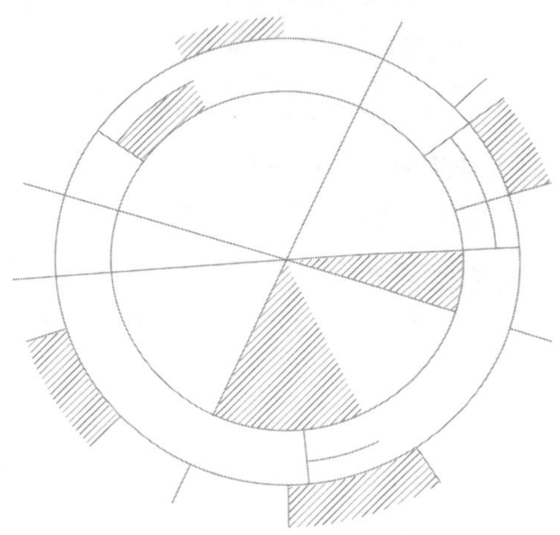

Chapter 7

Once again, we were all in the outpost's quad. A disheveled Buzz stood in front of us as the destroyed Armadillo smoldered nearby.

"What exactly . . ." a flabbergasted Buzz started, pointing at the dead robot beyond the hole in the wall. "How did that . . ."

He turned back to us, demanding, "Who *are* you?"

Well, the cat was out of the bag now. There was no point in hiding the fact we were only cadets and not real Zap Patrol officers.

I stood up from my spot on a crate and saluted him. "We're the Junior Patrol. At your service."

Darby scrunched her face and hocked a loogie.

A vine burst suddenly from the ground and grabbed my foot, tugging me off balance. Annoyed, I swatted it away, and it retreated underground. I stood back at attention quickly.

Buzz frowned. "Please elaborate."

"We're a volunteer team of self-motivated cadets . . . who train one weekend a month here at the outpost. Mo and Darby and I were the first to arrive last weekend when the robots showed up. So . . . we cooked up Operation Surprise Party," I explained.

Being in training didn't make us unfit for duty. Together as a team, we had taken down that robot. Well, except for Darby. But as she was honoring the terms of her parole, I'm certain she cheered us all on . . . in her own cranky way, from the sidelines. Plus, at least she was dedicated to following the rules. That was a very admirable quality to have!

Even Mo hadn't give up on trying something new. Sure, it might've taken a few harpoon spears to hit his target, but only one was needed to finish that robot off for good.

"I prefer Operation Puppet Master." Mo spoke

up with a shrug, using one hand to act as the Zurg ship and his other to cut at it. "We're gonna cut the strings to the robots."

"Oh, that's clever," Sox said, impressed.

"Guys! It's Operation Surprise Party! We already voted!" I reminded them.

"Not as good," Mo muttered under his breath.

Buzz sighed and nodded. "Do you have munitions training?" he asked.

"Partial," I admitted.

"Tactical engagement?"

"Not yet."

"Combat experience?" Buzz asked, hopeful.

Excitedly, I pointed at him. "Yes! If you count that robot situation we just went through."

"Okay," he said as if he'd seen enough, and walked to a nearby rover.

When he began to load in weapons, I stepped forward and asked, "What are you doing?"

"Look, I'm very supportive of your training initiatives. You seem like very nice people. But I'm gonna go ahead and take it from here," he replied.

His rejection stung a little, but I didn't flinch.

There were big mean things out to get all of us, and Operation Surprise Party was the solution to all our problems—including his.

"We just saved you from that robot," I reminded him.

Buzz stopped his task and looked at me. "Excuse me?"

"Mo made the kill shot," I said, pointing to Mo.

"Mo got lucky," Buzz said, unimpressed.

"Very," Mo agreed with a nod.

You're not supposed to agree with him, Mo!

After Buzz loaded in the last crates and closed the door, he said to us, "So . . . if you could just point me in the direction of another ship."

Mo said, "Oh, they have some old ships at the abandoned storage depot."

"Great, where's that?" Buzz asked.

"Oh, you can't miss it. It's over near the resource reconstituting center," I answered.

Buzz shook his head. "And where's that?"

"You know . . . right by where the old fabrication plant used to be," Darby added.

When he shook his head again, I realized that for the last twenty-two years, he and Sox had been in outer space. I remembered what Grandma had said to me before she brought me here to the Zap Patrol outpost for a tour:

A Space Ranger must map out their surroundings.

While they'd been in outer space, so much had changed.

Buzz didn't know his surroundings anymore.

"What *do* you know?" I asked curiously.

"I know the base," Buzz admitted.

A plan lit up inside my head, brighter than a thousand Star Command floodlights.

This was it! This was our chance to prove to Buzz Lightyear that he needed us, the Junior Patrol, as much as we needed him. Our home was still a foreign planet to him, and to win this war against the Zurg ship and its robots, he had to navigate the playing field.

And we, the Junior Patrol, would show him exactly how!

I held back my excitement and calmly said, "We'll just show you."

We all climbed into the rover.

Buzz drove, following my directions to the storage depot. I rode up front with him and with Sox in my lap. Mo and Darby were in the back with the crates Buzz had loaded while he was trying to ditch us.

As he steered, he still had a serious and determined look on his face. Then he started speaking into his wrist communicator.

"Buzz Lightyear supplemental mission log: Having finally achieved hyperspeed, I now have an additional obstacle in my way. In order to flee this planet, I'll have to destroy a massive alien ship," he said. "Alone, with no assistance of any kind."

He was planning on doing this without us, like his mind was already set on not giving us a chance.

It bothered me a little.

Okay, more than a little.

But I wasn't going to give up on proving to him how wrong he was about us.

"You know, we could help you. It *is* our plan," I said, stroking Sox's head.

Sounding very unconvinced, Buzz said, "I can't allow that. Star Command Code 27-0-9.3 forbids me from placing unqualified personnel in harm's way."

"Okay. But I'm a Hawthorne," I said confidently, pointing to my nameplate.

Buzz said, "There's more to it than a name, Izzy. You have to know exactly—"

Trying to finish his sentence, I spoke up: "What you're going to say next."

"How to react in any situation," he finished. Oops, I guessed it would take a little more getting to know each other before I could finish his sentences like Grandma did.

I shook my head. "I thought I had that one."

Buzz rolled his eyes and looked in the rearview mirror, shifting his attention to Darby.

"And you're in a correctional situation of some kind?" he asked her.

"Parole program. I do this and they shave a little time off my sentence," Darby admitted, then added sincerely, "But really I learned a lot in there."

"Darby can take any three things and make 'em explode," I boasted, hoping that would prove to him how resourceful we were.

Darby nodded knowingly.

"And what about you?" Buzz asked, moving on to Mo.

With a shrug, Mo said, "Me? Oh, I have a hard time sticking with things, so I thought I would give myself some forced structure. Signed up for this outfit and *instantly* regretted it. I mean, it was fun coming up with our little plan. That was cool. Didn't think we were actually going to do it."

I widened my eyes, shocked. "Wait, seriously?"

Mo pointed to the Zurg ship, saying to me, "How were *we* going to get up there and blow up a whole giant spaceship? Look at us."

Then he looked at Buzz. "But then *you* showed up, and I was like, 'Uh-oh.' So . . . honestly, I'm glad you're taking it from here."

Even though I appreciated Mo's honesty, I couldn't help shaking my head at his doubt in Operation Surprise Party (or Operation Puppet Master, depending on who you asked) and in me as the Junior Patrol leader. But it didn't hurt my feelings. It only motivated me to work a little harder to make him believe in me like I believed in him.

"Oh, on your right," I told Buzz, pointing to the storage depot.

He parked the rover, got out, and started to unload the crates onto a dolly.

"Hey, keep working on your skills. It's the only way you get better," he said encouragingly.

"We can help you," I said through the window.

"And I appreciate that," Buzz said, holding up the crystal, safe inside its canister.

Happiness lit up within me at his accepting our offer.

Yes, yes! My plan worked—

"Just go back to your training facility. Stay alert, stay safe," he continued, pointing at the storage depot. I deflated, realizing he wasn't inviting us

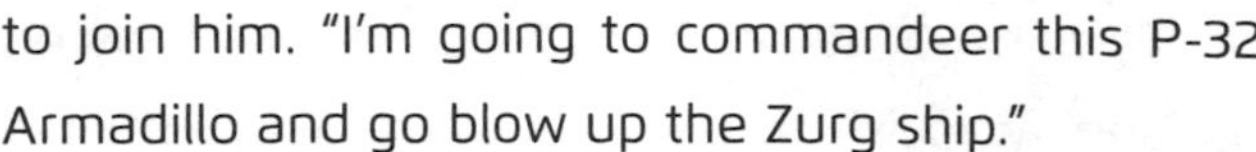

to join him. "I'm going to commandeer this P-32 Armadillo and go blow up the Zurg ship."

"So this is just goodbye?" I asked.

"Affirmative," Buzz replied.

I petted Sox's fuzzy head one last time before he leapt out the window and landed gracefully on his white paws.

Then Buzz closed the rover's back door on us.

Darby, Mo, and I watched him wheel the dolly into the storage depot with Sox following him. He didn't look back, turn around, or wave goodbye.

After everything we'd been through, he left us behind.

He didn't want our help, or us.

IZZY AND GRANDMA'S BLAST FROM THE PAST

Grandma's Office

I really liked school, because I got to learn and do cool things. I always sat up straight at my desk and paid extra-careful attention to what the teacher was saying. But right then, it was hard to stay focused, because Grandma had promised to take me to her commander office for the first time ever!

I kept looking at the clock and tapping my stylus pen on my tablet.

Thirty minutes to go!

"Well, Izzy?" my teacher, Mr. Cloud, said, crossing his arms.

I looked at him, then looked around. Everyone else's eyes were on me, too.

"Yes, sir?" I asked, a little embarrassed.

"How many planets are in the planetary system nearest ours?" he asked again. Oh, I read a whole book about this, and Dad even helped me make a model of all the planets. It wasn't for a school grade or anything. I just really liked making things.

"There are eight, sir," I answered.

He nodded, pleased. "Thank y—"

"There are also five dwarf planets," I added excitedly, smiling.

Just as I was about to tell the class how cold the farthest planet could get, Mr. Cloud said, "Thank you, Izzy. That's the perfect setup for the next part of today's lesson."

I slumped down in my seat. I had a lot more to say, but I guessed Mr. Cloud had the whole lesson planned already.

We watched a hologram video about how planetary systems worked. It showed us all about the orbit of planets around their sun, and how some planets even had their own moons. One night when I was supposed to be asleep, I overheard Mom and Dad talking about how much Grandma had loved her home planet, which was millions of light-years from T'Kani Prime. So the next day I made her a miniature planet as a surprise. Sometimes she looked up at the sky and would say she missed seeing her moon.

I thought maybe I should make her a mini moon, too, so her mini home planet wouldn't be alone.

After Mr. Cloud sent homework assignments to our school tablets, I stuffed my things into my backpack and ran out the door. Grandma waited for me out in the hallway like she promised.

I gave her a big hug, hopping up and down.

She laughed. "Someone's excited."

"Because we get to go to your office today, Grandma!" I exclaimed.

She took my hand, and we walked slowly down the corridor, because she had a little limp like she'd stubbed her toe.

"Are you okay, Grandma?" I asked, looking at her feet.

She looked down at me with a smile. "I'm just

getting old, sweetheart. All these Star Command missions are catching up to me."

A long time ago, Grandma flew to planetary systems all throughout space and explored planets there to see if they were safe enough for the scientific explorers like Grandma Kiko to come out of hypersleep inside the *Turnip* and explore the surface. Some planets had no life at all, and others had lots, but sometimes the alien plants and creatures weren't so friendly.

But now the *Turnip* was stuck in the middle of the Star Command base we lived on. Sometimes Grandma liked to joke that it grew roots so no one could pull it out.

It was cloudy outside. Lightning flashed by a mountain range far away, and thunder rumbled. Grandma said we needed to hurry or we'd get wet, so we climbed onto the back of a motor kart-truck and a nice lady drove us to headquarters.

Our legs dangled over the edge and I kicked, giggling with anticipation. When we got there, me and Grandma counted to three aloud before we jumped down.

"All right, Izzy," Grandma said, pointing to the entry door. "We have to be quiet as we walk through the building so everyone can concentrate on their jobs. So you know what that means, right?"

I nodded. "It's time to turn on our stealth mode."

"Exactly," Grandma said with a smile. She pressed an invisible button on her chest, and I did the same on myself. Then she took my hand and led me inside. Everyone who worked there looked so serious, doing their jobs in their blue uniforms and caps.

Two doors hissed open and some workers walked out.

My eyes went big as I saw the Mission Control room. There was a gigantic blue screen that stretched from wall to wall and desks with lots of computer screens and blinking buttons.

Then the doors shut.

"Whoa," I whispered in awe. Grandma must have heard me.

"Would you like to take a little detour, sweetheart?" Grandma whispered, and I nodded eagerly. She put her palm on a scanner and the doors opened back up.

She took me into the Mission Control room. On the huge blue screen, there was a planetary map like the one I studied in school, but this one was different. I saw T'Kani Prime, the other planets, and our star, Alpha T'Kani, but a spaceship-shaped symbol glowed on the screen, leaving behind lots of dots.

"Grandma, what's that?" I asked in a whisper, pointing to it.

"That's my friend Buzz, sweetheart," Grandma whispered back. "He's on his mission in space."

The spaceship symbol didn't move.

"Is he stuck up there?" I whispered.

"Time works differently for him, dear," Grandma whispered back. "Up there, he's going superfast, but down here, time is slow and steady."

Confused, I scrunched up my face.

"If he's going superfast, is he in a race?" I whispered. At school, I raced my friends all the time, but on the big wide screen, it looked like Buzz was in a race all by himself. That didn't look like much fun.

Grandma smiled. "Yes, he's in a race, and if he wins, everyone wins."

"Is there a prize, Grandma?" I whispered as she put her hands on my shoulders and guided me out of the room.

"Yes, sweetheart. The prize is going back to our home planet," she answered as we walked to her office.

"I learned about a new planet in school today. I know the names of all nine continents and all seven oceans," I whispered. Then I named them all. Grandma didn't stop me. She listened and told me I was a smart cookie. When we reached Grandma's office door, a man came up to us and saluted Grandma.

"Commander," he greeted.

"Captain Burnside, it's always nice to see you," Grandma said, looking to me. "Izzy, say hello."

I smiled at him, waving. "Hi, Captain Burnside."

"Hello, Izzy," he said with a nod, then asked Grandma, "Commander, have you thought any about my idea for a laser shield?"

"I'm still considering it, Captain. Lightyear is still on his mission, and if it's successful, we won't need a laser shield. It is a very good plan B to have if the bugs become more of a challenge for the Zap Patrol," Grandma said.

"Rule number three: Always be prepared for a challenge," I recited.

IZZY AND GRANDMA'S BLAST FROM THE PAST

Grandma patted my head lovingly and said, "Very good, Izzy."

She said goodbye to him and took me into her office.

"Whoa," I said, looking around. I ran over to the rug with the Star Command emblem on it. Next I went to the wide window to see the view of the base, the mudlands, and the mountains. Then I ran behind Grandma's desk to look at the corkboard with pinned pictures and the whiteboard filled with notes and numbers.

In the corner, I saw a *real* Space Ranger suit inside a glass case. I had only seen one in Grandma's old pictures.

"Oh!" I gasped, racing to it.

HAWTHORNE was on its nametag, and I swirled around to face Grandma.

"This is yours, Grandma?" I asked, pointing to it.

"It is," she admitted. "I keep it in here to remember the good times."

I dropped to my knees and pleaded, "Grandma, can I touch it, please, please, please?"

"Yes, you can," she agreed, holding up a finger. "As long as you're gentle."

I nodded, getting off the floor. "I promise to be super gentle."

After Grandma opened the glass case for me, I touched the boots, the legs, the empty blaster holster at the hips, the thick gloves, the wrist communicator, and the chest plate buttons.

"Grandma, what's that?" I asked, pointing to a red pull string.

"It's a surrender string. A Space Ranger only pulls it if they want to give up on their mission," Grandma said. "But remember, a Space Ranger always finishes the mission. Keep trying even if you're afraid. That's bravery."

"You can be brave and afraid, too?" I asked.

"You know what I think the *B* in plan B stands for?" Grandma asked.

I shook my head.

"Bravery, because when plan A didn't work, you didn't give up. You tried something else," Grandma said with a wink.

She took off her suit's helmet and asked, "Would you like to try it on, sweetheart?"

I nodded eagerly. "Yes, please!"

She placed it on me, and I looked like I was wearing an upside-down fishbowl. I looked silly, but I felt brave.

"Do you feel like a Space Ranger?" she asked.

I nodded, making the helmet bobble.

"When I get older and become a Space Ranger, can I wear your suit?" I asked.

"Of course, sweetheart. It's all yours," Grandma said.

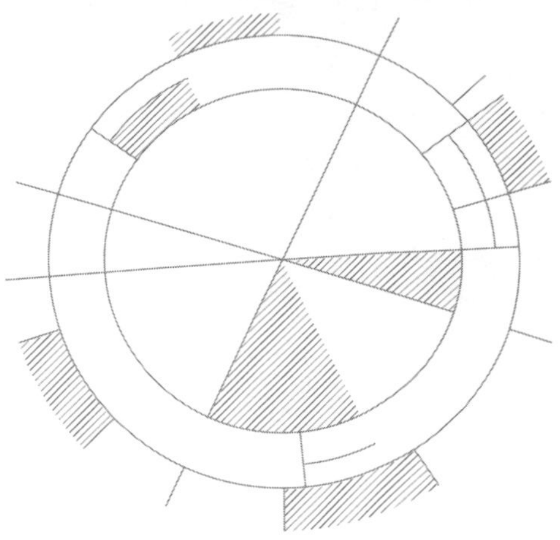

Chapter 8

"That went well," Darby said, shaking her head.

"It did?" Mo frowned, rubbing his bearded chin. "It looked like it went very badly to me."

Darby rolled her eyes and said, "I was being sarcastic."

"And I was being—" Mo started.

"Pessimistic?" Darby interrupted.

"Realistic," Mo said.

I clapped my hands together to get their attention. "I think we should all be optimistic. After all this time, Buzz Lightyear is back."

If only Grandma were here to see that for herself.

Pointing to the abandoned storage depot, I said, "Operation Surprise Party needed a pilot, and he's in there."

For two decades, everyone believed he had died in space, but even before he stole a spaceship and rocketed off T'Kani Prime, people had stopped believing in him.

Except Grandma.

She made him promise to complete his mission.

But she had given me a mission of my own, and I couldn't let her down. In my head, I recited the three rules she had given me:

Rule #1: Never stop believing in yourself.

Rule #2: Always believe in the best of people, even if they don't believe in themselves.

Rule #3: Always be prepared for a challenge.

I believed in myself. For my entire life, I'd studied and trained for this.

Even though Darby couldn't touch weapons, pick locks, or make things explode because of her parole, I believed in her. Even though Mo didn't have very good aim and was still trying to figure out who he wanted to be, I believed in him, too.

The only one who didn't believe in any of us was Buzz. We had lasted this long without him—before the robots and after the robots. That had to count for something! We had to prove to Buzz Lightyear that the impossible was possible as long as we worked as a team.

If I drove the rover to the other side of the storage depot and *temporarily* blocked Buzz's path for takeoff, we could force him to at least hear us out . . . *again*.

I climbed over into the driver's seat and put my hands on the steering wheel, ready to rev my plan into action. But . . . I couldn't drive anywhere without keys.

"Mo, can I have the keys?" I asked.

"I'm not the one who drove here, remember?"

We all looked at the storage depot again.

"Buzz has got the keys, doesn't he?" Darby asked.

I nodded slowly and sighed. "Yuuuuuup."

"And we have to go get them, don't we?" Darby asked.

"Yuuuuuup," I said again.

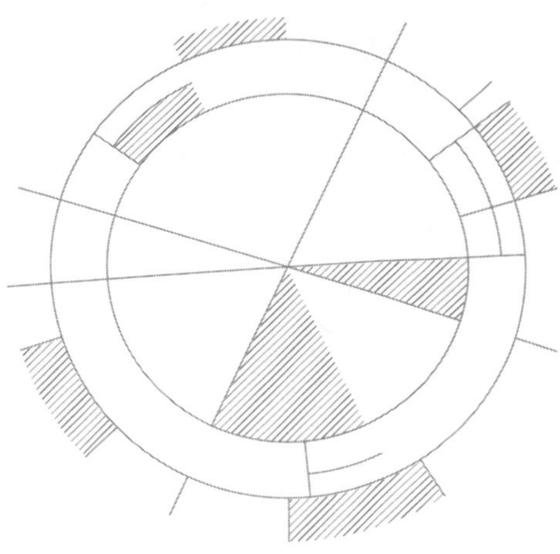

Chapter 9

After climbing out of the rover, we walked toward the storage depot.

"Operation Surprise Party is still on," I reminded Mo and Darby.

Mo pretended to slice invisible puppet strings with his hands. "Looks to me like Buzz wants to *cut* the puppet strings on his own."

"We *voted* on Operation Surprise Party, remember? Nobody likes Operation Puppet Master except you," Darby said grumpily, glaring at him.

Cocking his chin up, Mo said proudly, "Well, the robot cat liked it. He said it was clever."

Darby began, "He said Operation Puppet Master was clever, not y—"

Mo and I jumped back as a vine lurched from the muddy ground and coiled around Darby's ankle, yanking at her. She fell and landed on her bottom, then kicked at the vine until it retreated underground again.

Mo hunched over, laughing at her—until a vine wrapped around his waist and tugged him down, dragging his butt through the mud.

"Ah, ah, ahhh!" he said, flailing and struggling.

Now it was Darby's turn to laugh.

I ran over to Mo and wrangled the squirmy vine off him, growling. It gave up, slithering back into the ground.

Putting my hands on my hips, I glanced between the two of them, disappointed.

"Guys, even though *we voted on a name*," I started, looking at Mo briefly, "the name doesn't matter—the mission does. The circumstances might be . . . less than ideal, but in times like these, we need to follow Grandma Rule Number Three, which is . . ."

"'Always be prepared for a challenge,'" Mo and Darby recited unenthusiastically as they picked themselves up off the ground.

"Exactly!" I said, smiling at them like a proud teacher. "Now let's face this challenge head-on, team."

We entered the storage depot's creepy darkness. Luckily, sunlight poured from the scattered overhead skylights. Forklifts had been left in places they shouldn't have been. Crates, weapons, and supplies weren't in the right places, either. It looked like the depot workers had left everything where it was when the sirens sounded and the Zurg ship arrived. The place looked empty, but it didn't feel empty. It felt like something was watching us. I shrugged off the feeling. We had to find Buzz to get those keys back so we could continue on our mission, with or without Buzz.

In the distance, I heard voices. I looked at Mo and Darby and pointed toward the sound. It seemed to be coming from a fenced-in locker area. "I think they're this way."

The quicker we found Buzz, the quicker we could start Operation Surprise Party up again.

By the time we got there, he had geared up in a Space Ranger suit and was looking down at it in admiration.

"Fits like a glove," he said, smiling to himself.

He looked so happy. It was like watching two long-lost friends reunite. He struck a pose, arms in a heroic position. Then another, more elaborate pose, again and again. It was kind of funny, actually, but I tried not to laugh. I didn't want to ruin his moment.

Finally, he turned and saw us. He startled, clearly surprised that we were back so soon.

I smiled at him sheepishly. "Sorry to interrupt. Looks like you were having a real nice moment."

"What are you doing here?" Buzz demanded to know.

"Uh, you took the keys to our truck," Mo said.

Buzz sighed. "Okay, my apologies."

He went to his old suit and fished out the keys.

I opened my mouth, prepared to give him a detailed oral report on the team's best strengths and qualities—

"Here. Now off you go," he said, tossing them to Mo.

But they bounced off Mo's open palm and hit the ground. And the ground hit the alarm button on the keys, triggering the truck's blaring sirens and honking horn all the way outside the depot. The sound echoed around us.

Mo quickly scooped up the keys and fumbled with them.

Buzz whispered loudly, "Shh! Shh! Quiet! Turn it off!"

"I'm trying," Mo grumbled, attempting to press the off button with his gloved fingers. "Ha!"

Mo's *ha* wasn't a funny-fun-fun *ha* but a nervous, panicky *ha*.

That looks-empty-but-doesn't-feel-empty hunch came back to me as I heard loud buzzing overhead. When the workers abandoned the storage depot to get back to the base, the bugs must've thought it was a good place to hide from the laser-firing robots stomping around.

The bugs had turned the storage depot into a slumber party, and we woke them up.

And this was a party we weren't invited to!

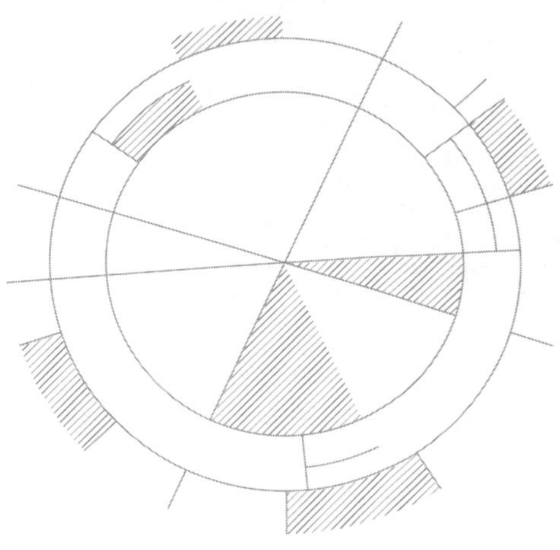

Chapter 10

The swarm of bugs zoomed toward the locker room.

"Somebody get—" Buzz started, but I was already slamming the door shut. We heard loud, heavy thunks as the bugs slammed against the door, trying to get in.

"The door," I finished for him, then laughed. "Way ahead of you!"

Mo finally pressed the right button, and the noisy truck went silent. But I much preferred the sirens and the honking over the sounds of very cranky bugs crawling and flying around outside the locker room.

"Well, I'm going to be blunt here," Mo said, looking down at the keys. "I wish that hadn't happened."

"So do the rest of us!" Darby yelled, putting her hands on her hips.

"It's okay. We can get out of this," I said. Then, to myself, I added, "Just think like a Hawthorne."

Being a Hawthorne meant being resourceful. It meant thinking about what Grandma would do in this situation. There had to be something in here that could help us evade the bugs. I glanced around the locker room and spotted three more Space Ranger suits.

Perfect!

Buzz grabbed a weapon from the squeaky dolly and instructed us each to grab one, too.

Darby held up her hands and said, "Boy, I'd love to, but my parole—"

"As a Star Command officer, I grant you emergency authority," Buzz said, serious. "We're going to blast our way out of here."

Darby smiled and grabbed the biggest weapon. "Now we're talking."

Sox then said, "Buzz, the probability of surviving a frontal attack is thirty-eight point two percent."

Mo frowned, looking at the door that kept *thunk-thunk-thunk*ing angrily. "Seems a bit low."

The less-than-stellar news didn't stop a plan from popping into my head.

I pointed to Buzz's green chest plate. "What about stealth mode?"

Buzz looked at me, surprised. "How do you know about stealth mode?"

"Grandma and I used to play stealth mode all the time. It was like hide-and-seek, but with a twist," I told him proudly.

Buzz nodded. "Okay, well, it's actually good thinking. I'll use stealth mode to disorient them."

I pointed to the other Space Ranger suits. "Or . . . and stick with me here . . . we could *all* use stealth mode and just walk right out."

Buzz looked at the suits, then back at us. He frowned as Mo and Darby began to look through the gear.

"You mean *you* would wear Space Ranger suits?" he asked.

I pointed to the name tag on one of the suits. "This one already has my name on it."

The shiny name tag had my last name, Hawthorne, on it. Deep down, I knew it was Grandma's suit. When her office became

Commander Burnside's, her suit had been put away into storage.

It had been here so long there was dust on it now.

Buzz considered my plan, then sighed heavily.

A few minutes later, we'd all donned Space Ranger suits. Buzz stood in front of us like a general preparing to lead us into battle. Mo checked out his suit, pointing at the nameplate on it.

"Look, I'm Feathers . . . Featherins . . . Featherings . . ." he said, trying to read the last name upside down. Then something better caught his attention.

He pulled a small pen from his suit's chest plate. "Oh, look, a pen! Cool!" Mo looked around at the rest of us, asking excitedly, "Does yours have a pen?"

Buzz pushed the pen back into Mo's suit as he walked in front of our lineup.

"Okay, pay attention," Buzz commanded, making us stand a little straighter. "Stealth mode is fairly simple. There are just two parts. You press the button—"

Mo interrupted, pointing to a button on his suit's chest plate. "Is it this button?"

"I will tell you which button," Buzz promised.

Mo pointed to another and asked, "What about this button?"

"I'm sorry. We're not going to have time to go over all the buttons," Buzz said.

"Okay, forget about the button. What about this thing? It's more of a pull," Mo said, reaching for a red pull on his chest.

My jaw dropped in panic. When I was little, Grandma told me a Space Ranger only yanked their surrender string if they wanted to give up.

And a Space Ranger *never* gives up.

Buzz widened his eyes. "No, no, no!"

"No, no, no, don't—" I panicked, shaking my head.

Buzz grabbed Mo's hand in the nick of time. "That's the surrender string. You never pull that."

"There's no more shameful maneuver for a Space Ranger," I added, sagging in relief it hadn't been pulled.

"Did I miss which button is the stealth mode button?" Darby asked.

Frustrated, Buzz pointed out the correct button. "It's this button."

As Mo went to press it, Buzz ordered quickly, "Not yet!"

Mo froze like a statue as Buzz continued, "You

push *this* button. Then you go out the front door. I'll get on the Armadillo and go blow up this alien ship . . . and I'll see you on the *Turnip* when we're all heading home. Ready?"

I nodded. "Ready."

Darby nodded, too. "Ready."

"Ready," Mo said. Then his eyes grew big. "Wait!"

He hustled back to his discarded pants, dug out the truck keys, and dangled them above his head. "That would have been embarrassing."

"Okay," Buzz said, sighing loudly. "Goodbye again."

We all pressed the buttons on our suits, activating our stealth bubbles.

Stealth-mode Buzz opened the locker room door and wheeled the dolly over to the Armadillo. It seemed like the door and the dolly were being pushed by a ghost.

While he quietly inserted the hyperspeed crystal into the Armadillo's fuel panel, we slowly tiptoed past the bugs.

I held my breath, afraid the greedy insects would hear me if I didn't.

"Hey," Mo whispered. "Didn't he say there were two parts to stealth mode?"

"Shh! Shut it!" Darby hushed him grumpily, but Mo ignored her.

"He said first part, press the button . . . but then he never said the second part. Did he?" he continued quietly. Even though he should very much not have been talking, he did have an excellent point.

What was the second part to stealth mode?

Mo gasped in shock, pointing to Darby. "Wait. I can see you."

Darby widened her eyes. "I can see you, too!"

If they could see each other, that meant—

"The bugs can see us!" I exclaimed as the swarm of bugs crawled toward us.

"No, no, no!" a panicked Mo said as he yanked his suit's surrender string. He announced loudly, "I surrender!"

His suit puffed up like a plump raspberry. Bright emergency lights blinked and flashed within each inflated bulb.

Darby and I grabbed him and rolled him to the closest door.

"Back! Hey! Get back!" Darby shouted at the creepy-crawly creatures as if they'd actually listen to her.

I looked at no-longer-stealth-mode Buzz and the Armadillo, yelling at him, "This isn't working!"

"You have to keep going!" he shouted.

"We have to turn around!" I shouted at the same time as Darby and I turned around, rolling Mo toward the Armadillo.

As Sox watched us, he said something to Buzz.

Buzz then gave us his full attention, waving his arms in protest. "No, no! Don't come over here!"

But with the angry bugs at our heels, nothing—not even Buzz—could stop us from dashing to the Armadillo. Darby and I leapt through the ship's door, but puffy Mo couldn't fit. Buzz pulled the release on Mo's suit, causing it to deflate like a balloon so Buzz could tug him inside.

Buzz slammed the door shut behind him, and I sagged into my seat. We'd done it! We had made it onto a ship.

We were on our way to Operation Surprise Party!

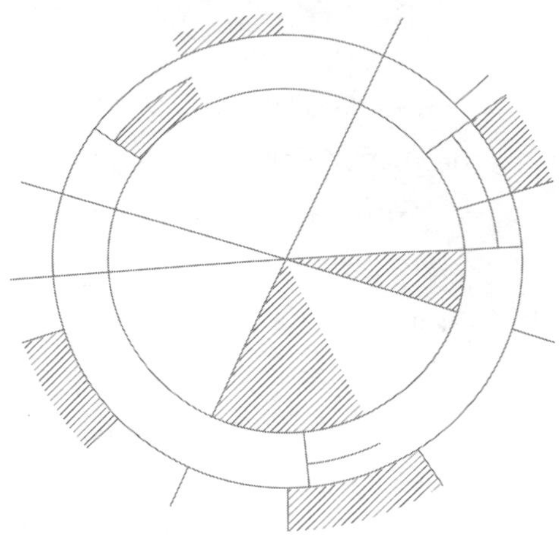

Chapter 11

"Whew. All right, all right! Way to adapt, team!" I said proudly.

Unamused, Buzz watched us give each other high fives. "Why are you congratulating yourselves? This was not the plan!"

"Because I Hawthorned us right out of that situation," I said, pointing to Grandma's nameplate on Grandma's suit. In that moment, it felt like mine.

Buzz lectured, "But you could have made it if—"

"You forgot to tell us the second part of the stealth mode," Mo reminded him.

"Well," Buzz said without further argument.

We all knew it was true, but now wasn't the time to talk it out. The bugs swarmed the Armadillo, cluttering the windshield and thudding against the hull outside.

"Okay, fine. Everyone just strap in," Buzz said, resigned.

As we took our seats and buckled up, he climbed into the captain's chair and turned on the engines. The Armadillo rumbled to life, and he flipped switches like an old pro, making the ship lift off the ground and hover.

Our bodies jerked back into our seats as the Armadillo blasted forward, crashing through the storage depot's glass windows. Not even that could unglue the bugs from the windshield. It was almost impossible to see outside.

"Hold on!" Buzz yelled, pushing a button that made the rear engines shoot out fire and lift us into the sky. We soared up and up and up, and my heart pounded loud in my ears like a drum as I realized—

"Are we going to space?" I asked worriedly.

"No, I'm going to drop you off somewhere," Buzz promised as he maneuvered the Armadillo into a barrel roll to shake the bugs off. My dizzy brain felt like it was doing a barrel roll in my head, too.

"Oh, that was a big swirly-doo. I think I'm going to vomit," Mo groaned, puffing out his cheeks like he'd do it any second.

"No, no! Do *not* vomit inside the vehicle!" Buzz ordered.

While Buzz bickered with Mo, I couldn't tear my eyes away from the window beside me as the blue sky got less blue and more outer-spacey black. Fear pumped through me. My chest tightened and my eyes widened.

I pointed a shaky finger to the window. "I can see stars! That is space!"

And we were getting closer to it.

Too close to it.

This was bad.

Very, very bad.

Buzz asked worriedly, "What is happening right now?"

"Umm, she's afraid of space," Darby informed him.

"What?" Buzz said, shocked. I knew it didn't make sense. I'd said I wanted to be a Space Ranger, and Space Rangers usually went to space.

But when I looked out, the only thing separating me from the endless, endless, endless blackness was a glass window.

Feeling even dizzier than when the Armadillo had done a barrel roll, I turned away from the sight, forgetting how to breathe.

"Izzy, remember your exercises," Darby reminded me.

The ones Grandma had taught me.

Deep breath in, breathe out.

Deep breath in, breathe out.

Deep breath in, breathe out.

Worry hit me like a missile. I was supposed to be brave, but space was a colossal giant I couldn't fight back against. How could I do this mission if the thought of space sent me running for the hills?

Sounding nauseated, Mo said groggily, "I think I need a bag."

"No, no, no, no! Engage your helmet! That'll catch it," Buzz ordered.

I widened my eyes, pointing to the windshield as I noticed—

"Buzz!" I shouted.

"Izzy! You just have to—" Buzz started.

"Look out!" I screamed as a sleek fighter

spaceship fired at the Armadillo. Buzz jerked the controls to swerve us out of the way. The enemy ship chased us across the sky. I'd never seen that ship before. Had the Zurg ship sent it after us?

"What is that?" a dumbfounded Buzz asked, steering the Armadillo hard to avoid getting hit again. Our bodies shook in our seats as something very big collided with the Armadillo, knocking us off course.

"We are hit!" Sox announced, shocked.

The Armadillo descended quickly, speeding through the gray skies and right into a pitch blackness I feared.

IZZY AND GRANDMA'S BLAST FROM THE PAST

The Mines

In my dream, I floated in space with Grandma. She had on her Space Ranger suit from the glass case in her Star Command office, and I had one that looked just like hers. Burning stars and colorful planets hovered all around us. The *Turnip* was there, waiting for us so we could go back to our home planet.

But me and Grandma were waiting for her friend Buzz Lightyear to join us so we could all leave together. While we waited for him, she held my hand and taught me all kinds of cool maneuvers, like flipping and doing cartwheels. There's no water in space, but she taught me how to swim, too, and we doggy-paddled to be silly.

"Oh, there he is," Dream Grandma said, pointing to a lumpy gray asteroid and its trail of fire and smoke zooming toward us. Buzz Lightyear surfed on top of it, waving.

Suddenly, the asteroid spiraled out of control, making Buzz stumble and fall.

Grandma tried to get us out of the way, but we got knocked apart.

"Izzy!" Dream Grandma yelled, reaching for me as I drifted away from her.

"Grandma!" I yelled back, trying to grab her hand.

But we floated farther and farther apart from each other. I tried to kick toward her, but it didn't work. Nothing I did worked. Soon Grandma and the *Turnip* looked more and more like little dots as I floated far, far away from them, the stars, and the planets until nothing but darkness was around me.

"Izzy," the dark whispered in Mom's voice and shook me. *"Izzy, wake up."*

I woke up with a scream. My heart pounded hard. My parents stood beside my bed, and Mom's hand shook my shoulder.

"Sweetheart, it was only a nightmare," Mom said, sitting on my bed. She hugged me and rubbed my back. My throat hurt from screaming, so Dad went into the kitchen and got me some water. I gulped it down, and Mom tucked me back into bed.

They both kissed me good night, and at the door, Dad said, "Sweet dreams, kiddo. You've got a big day ahead of you tomorrow."

The next day, me and Grandma were going to T'Kani Prime's Dark Side to visit the mines. But I didn't have sweet dreams, because I was too afraid to go to sleep. I didn't want to lose Grandma again.

At breakfast, I dozed off at the table and my face fell into my food.

"Izzy," Mom said, gently shaking me awake. "Izzy, wake up."

I woke up with a loud yawn and looked at my breakfast sleepily. All our meals at the Star Command base came in rectangular boxes. Most of our food looked like different-colored triangles, and each color had a different flavor. They didn't taste bad, but juicy sandwiches were the best to eat.

"Maybe we should postpone your field trip until you've rested up," Dad said, peeling a green triangle of food off my cheek.

"No!" I gasped, waking up completely. "I'm up, I'm up!"

After I gobbled down the rest of my breakfast, Dad helped me into my puffy snowsuit and snow boots. I had to wear fuzzy earmuffs and thick mittens, too. The Dark Side had no sun, which meant it was extra cold and it snowed. Dad wrapped a scarf around my neck over and over until it covered my nose and mouth, too.

"You ready?" he asked. I tried to say, *Yes, sir,* but the scarf over my mouth made it sound like *Mes, thir.*

"Good morning, sweetheart," Grandma greeted me, wearing her own snowsuit. It wasn't as puffy as mine. She stood by the Armadillo ship. The last time I saw one was when we visited the Zap Patrol outpost. I begged her to let me ride in one, and she promised me I could.

That's what I loved about Grandma. She always kept her promises no matter what.

"Rood rorning, Frandma," I said through my scarf.

We waved goodbye to Dad and climbed into the Armadillo. Grandma walked into the cockpit, patted the copilot seat, and told me to sit there. I waddled into the cockpit and hopped in the seat excitedly. I tried to buckle my seat belt, but my gloves wouldn't let me.

Grandma laughed and helped me buckle up, then sat in the pilot seat. She put on a pair of glasses and started up the engines.

Surprised, I pulled down my scarf to ask, "Grandma, *you're* gonna fly there?"

Grandma gave me a nod and a wink and flew us away.

"Whoa," I said, looking out the window to

see the brown mudlands around the base. We flew miles and miles over the green treetops. I even saw the Zap Patrol outpost and the storage depot. Everyone looked like busy little bugs down there.

The sky turned darker and darker even though the day had just started.

"This is the Dark Side, Izzy. Our sun, Alpha T'Kani, doesn't come to this side of the planet," Grandma said as she flew the Armadillo into the dimming light. It reminded me of my nightmare, and for a moment I wanted to ask her to turn back around. But I didn't. I didn't want her to know I was afraid.

I hunkered down in my seat, not wanting to look out the window anymore.

Then Grandma said happily, "Oh, you have to see this, Izzy!"

Afraid, I craned my neck to peep down below at the pools of red-hot lava spitting out fire and steam like volcanos.

IZZY AND GRANDMA'S BLAST FROM THE PAST

"That's the fire geysers!" I gasped as they erupted. Down there, the fire geysers glowed and it didn't look so dark anymore. But when the Armadillo left them behind, I stopped looking out the window again. When we got to the mines, Grandma landed the Armadillo by a glass building that glowed bright like a flashlight.

Grandma helped me with my seat belt, and when she opened the door, a blast of cold air hit us. I hopped out and my boots went *thunk* on the frozen ground. My breath looked like clouds as I shivered and hugged myself.

"That's the command center, Izzy," Grandma said, pointing to the glow-in-the-dark building. I stared up at the black sky and froze, afraid. Even though I was wide awake, my nightmare came back to me. My heart raced, my chest ached, and I waddled back to the Armadillo and hurried in.

"Izzy," Grandma called after me. "Izzy!"

My boots made me trip, and I fell, but I didn't

get back up. I curled into a ball and closed my eyes. Grandma got back in the Armadillo.

"Sweetheart, what's wrong?" she asked, kneeling by me.

"I want to go home," I cried. "I'm scared."

"What are you scared of?" she asked.

The door was still open, and I pointed a finger at the dark outside.

"I don't want to float away," I said. "I don't want to be lost forever."

"Oh, sweetheart, we all get scared and overwhelmed sometimes. It's okay to feel that way."

She hugged me, but I was so afraid I kept shaking.

"Breathe in," she instructed softly, and I did it.

"Now breathe out," she said, and I did that, too.

"Breathe in," she repeated. "Breathe out."

I kept doing it over and over until my tears stopped.

But my fear wouldn't go away.

"Do you feel better?" Grandma asked.

"A little," I said back.

"Whenever you feel like that, breathe in and out like I showed you," she said, rubbing my back. "Okay, sweetheart?"

I nodded and snuggled into her.

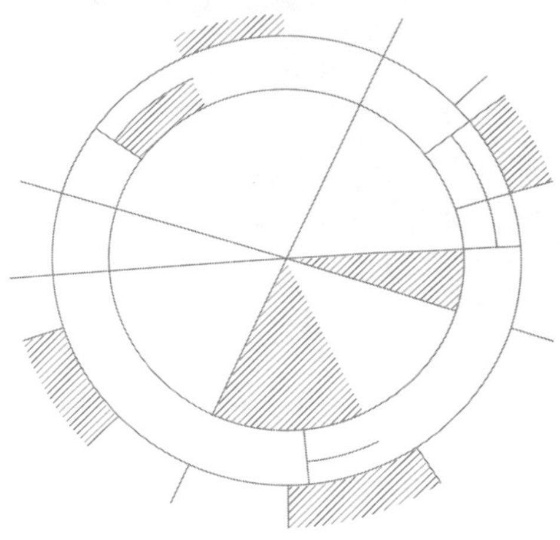

Chapter 12

"There's nothing! I can't see anything!" Buzz shouted.

"Oh, no, the Dark Side!" I yelled, gripping the armrests of my seat.

Sox spun his head around and around, then stopped with wide eyes.

"Oh! Over there! Ten o'clock!" he told Buzz.

Buzz clocked the bright lights and glowing fires of the mining operation in a vast crater, steering us in that direction.

"Hold on! This isn't gonna be pretty!" he exclaimed as he pulled on the controls to make the Armadillo do a steep nosedive. Gritting my teeth, I braced myself as the ship slammed hard into the ground, sending a plume of gray dust into the air.

We all caught our breath.

"Is everyone okay?" Buzz asked, stunned, like he couldn't believe we had survived a sky-high speed chase.

Who was I kidding? I couldn't believe it, either.

"I think so," I panted, shaking all over. Once the dust settled, Buzz stared into the inky black skies, probably trying to spot the enemy ship that had swatted us off course. Quietly, he stood up. His boots thumped as he reached the door and climbed out with Sox following him.

"Sox, get me a damage report," I heard him say outside the ship.

"Scanning. One moment, please," Sox said back, then made computing noises.

Darby, Mo, and I unbuckled our seat belts and joined them outside. I squatted down, gladder than glad to be back on the ground and not up there.

"Okay, this is better," I sighed, relieved.

Buzz frowned, looking down at me. "*This* is better?"

"No. Obviously, this is worse overall. I just meant . . ." I paused, pointing at the inky blackness of space up above. "You know. . . ."

I gulped, thinking about how we had nearly sailed into it. Being on the Dark Side of T'Kani Prime didn't ease my fears, either. The empty dark was all around us for miles and miles and miles. I couldn't run from it even if I wanted to.

"Wait, how are you afraid of space?" Buzz asked, confused.

"Oh, it's pretty easy. Did you know if you let go out there, you just keep going in that direction? *Forever*. Just . . ." I trailed off, using my hands to enact drifting far, far, far into space.

The more I thought about it, the more it freaked me out.

"Then how were you going to go blow up the alien ship?" Buzz asked.

"Oh, I would have been ground support," I said, a little embarrassed. "I know Grandma wasn't afraid of space."

"No. Because she was a *Space* Ranger," Buzz emphasized. "Astrophobia is an automatic disqualification."

Though wanting to be a Space Ranger and having a phobia of space was a bad combo, there had to be a way for me to achieve my dream and continue the Hawthorne legacy.

Darby gazed up at the night sky. "What was that thing?"

"I don't know," Buzz admitted.

"Well, is it going to come back?" Mo asked.

"I don't know," Buzz repeated, a little irritated this time.

"But how did it—" I started, but he shot me a stern look. "Okay, yeah. You don't know."

We all looked out at the Dark Side's cold, barren landscape of rugged mountains and deep craters. The more I stared, the more hopeless I felt. We had Buzz, but having Buzz didn't mean much if none of us knew what to do next.

Rule #3: Always be prepared for a challenge.

Grandma always had a plan A, B, and C to handle any challenge.

Buzz marched over to the Armadillo and opened the fuel panel door, then removed his spiky glowing crystal and its canister. "I was done. I finally had the crystal. This was supposed to be over. But who am I kidding? I need a time machine."

I wanted to tell him he was wrong. He didn't need a time machine. He just needed us. If only he would have trusted me.

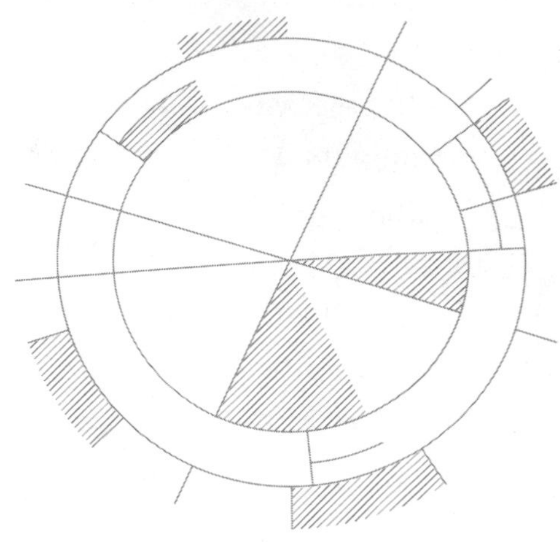

Chapter 13

"Assessment complete," Sox announced, coming back from his trip around the Armadillo.

"How bad is it?" Buzz asked, arching his eyebrow.

Sox's eyes projected a holographic model of the Armadillo. "The blast was absorbed by the heat shield and only caused a minor electrical short."

That didn't sound so bad—whatever it meant.

"Okay . . ." Buzz trailed off.

"So in order to be flight operational, the Armadillo will require a material of specialized capacitance," Sox informed Buzz. He wanted the robotic cat to continue explaining, but Sox just stared at him, marking the end of the damage report.

Buzz asked, "Well, what does that mean?"

"You know, like electrical stuff," Mo said.

Buzz sighed. "Okay. Thank you."

While he walked over to the Armadillo and pulled open a panel, Mo said to me and Darby, "We learned about this. Specialized capacitance? Remember, we built those field radios last month."

I smiled at the memory. "Oh, yeah. That was fun."

"Yeah, Darby messed hers up," Mo said, jerking a thumb at Darby.

Darby glared at him. "I'm gonna mess *you* up."

Buzz turned to us, looking annoyed. "Please, I'm trying to think here."

We gathered around, whispering to each other.

"I messed mine up, but then I fixed it!" Darby said matter-of-factly.

"Yeah, but you broke that computer console," I reminded her.

"I needed that little coil thing for its . . . What was it?" Darby asked.

"Specialized capacitance," Mo finished.

Buzz addressed us again, looking more annoyed than the last time. "Hey! Honestly, there's a lot of room out there. If you want to reminisce, you can go," he said, pointing to an area far away from him, "over there. Or look!"

He pointed again in a different direction—once again to an area far, far away from him. "There's no one trying to think over there."

I pointed to the glow of the mining facility. "We can go up there!"

"Fine. Perfect," Buzz said, turning back to the Armadillo.

An inkling of an idea struck me like a lightning bolt and I nodded as it grew and grew and grew into—

"Yes!" I clapped my hands. "Okay, new plan!"

Buzz frowned. "What?"

"The mining facility will have a console, right? That console will have a little coil thing, right? And that little coil thing will have the . . ." I paused, aiming a finger at Mo for him to finish my sentence.

"Specialized capacitance," Mo filled in.

"That we need to fix the ship," I went on. "Right?"

Buzz blinked, turning to his robotic cat. "Sox?"

"She's right," Sox replied.

Buzz nodded, thinking over my plan. I smiled, because I knew that he knew that my plan was a good one. It was a plan even Grandma would approve. A plan Grandma would've thought up herself.

"Well, look at that," Buzz said, hesitant. "Good . . . job. Huh. Then let's go get that part . . . and then get out of here."

He looked up at the dark skies. "Before that thing finds us again."

We deployed our helmets, and lights lit up around our faces to help us see in the dark. As we trudged up the rocky hill dusted in frost, there were poles with bright light bulbs to help us, too. Snowflakes came down and cold wind blew. The cool thing about Space Ranger suits was that they were insulated, which basically meant they kept us warm so we didn't turn into icicles. I didn't need a bulky scarf this time around.

We reached the crest of the rocky hill and gazed down at the enormous mining operation. Machinery had carved out terraced bowls that looked like levels and levels of ledges. The abandoned mining bots scurried in and out of the tunnels. They stuck to their task, burrowing away like there wasn't an alien invasion happening.

"Whoa," Buzz said, his face full of awe. "We can probably find a coil in there."

If he was impressed now, I bet he'd be even more impressed by the miners and bots working side by side. Though I wasn't a fan of the Dark Side, whenever I volunteered in the mines, the sense of community thriving in the darkest of places made me happy and proud.

Even though we were stuck on a planet with mean squirmy vines, man-eating bugs, and lots of other unfriendly things, we stayed hopeful in a hopeless situation. This mine, the Zap Patrol outpost, and the base were all Grandma's plan Bs. If she couldn't go back home, she would make this planet work just as well.

We trekked on and on until we reached the mine's glassed-in command center, located at the very edge of a crater's cliff. It was supported by angled stilts that kept it from falling over.

Buzz cleared his throat and started speaking into his wrist communicator.

"Buzz Lightyear mission log: In order to repair our ship, we have to find some way to get inside this command center and—"

Just then, the command center opened. While Buzz was busy recording his thoughts, Darby had hot-wired the entry pad.

"Nice job, elderly convict," Buzz said, impressed.

"That may have been a violation of my parole," Darby mumbled.

We all entered the command center. Our boots clanked on the floors as we walked down a short hall, which led to the command center's main room. Sox strolled to the large control panel filled with buttons, levers, and screens.

"Okay, the coil should be in here," I said, pointing to the console.

"Sox?" Buzz asked. Sox crawled underneath the equipment.

"Need a pen?" Mo asked Sox.

"No, I'm fine."

Soon we heard the whirling sound of an electric screwdriver.

"And . . . got it!" Sox concluded, popping out from underneath the console with a coil in his mouth. Buzz squatted down and took it from him.

"Oh, good. That was easy," Buzz said.

"Okay, yeah, another time," Mo said. He pocketed his pen, but as he did so, his elbow hit a large red button on the wall.

Warning lights flashed.

Uh-oh. That wasn't good.

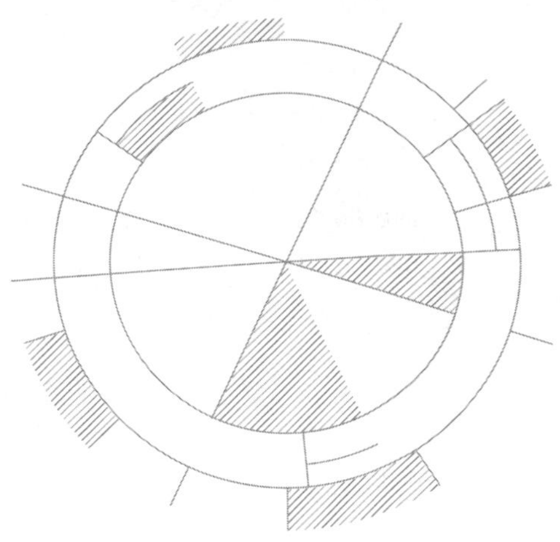

Chapter 14

"What did you do?" Darby asked Mo. Just then, the door slammed and a red laser cone appeared around each of us.

"Security measures activated," the security system announced.

"Whoa, what?" Darby shouted.

Buzz pushed against his cone, but it moved with him.

"What is this?" he shouted. We all tried walking around, but the cones stayed with us. We couldn't escape them!

"No! I'm not going to be locked up again!" Darby said. She ran toward the door and tried to press the button to open it, but she couldn't reach it from inside her cone. She threw herself at the button, shouting loudly, "No! No! NO!"

On her final lunge, Darby's cone bumped against the button, and the door opened with a loud beep.

"Okay," Darby said, relieved. "Okay."

I held my breath as she tried to walk through the door, but the cone held her back. She looked like a puppet, her body pushing against the cone that wouldn't let her leave.

I gulped. This was going to be a problem. We needed a plan to get out of these cones. Before I could say anything, Mo tried running through the exit, but his cone combined with Darby's as soon as they touched. They were trapped together!

"What did you do?" Darby asked.

Mo looked defensive. "I just tried to get past you!"

The door beeped again before closing.

"Aw, come on!" Darby shouted. She tried to open it again, but she couldn't get close enough to press the button. Mo was standing still and holding the cone back. She looked at him, frustrated. "Could you help me out here?"

"Me?" he asked. "Uh, yeah, all right."

The two of them threw their bodies at the

button, and together, they were able to press it and open the door. But their momentum sent them stumbling back.

"No, no, no, no!" I shouted as they flew toward me. Next thing I knew, I was squashed inside the same cone as Mo, Darby, and Sox. Sox meowed loudly as the door beeped and closed once again.

We all looked at the door and swiveled our heads to look at Buzz, who was still standing in his own security cone.

"Stay away from me!" he shouted.

"How are we going to get out of here?" I asked.

"Well, I don't know, but just stay away! I'm no help to anyone if I'm stuck in there with you." Buzz looked at the coil in his hand and sighed loudly before slipping it into his pocket. "Okay, let's think about it."

But I was already thinking of a new plan.

"Wait," I said. "There's a soft spot in the floor here. Maybe we can—"

"That's my foot!" Darby said.

"Oh, sorry." Oops. I guessed that wasn't going to help us get out of here. There had to be something else we could do.

"Um, this isn't our most pressing issue," Mo

said, "but worth mentioning . . . I have to go to the bathroom."

"What? How bad?" Darby asked.

"Bad enough to bring it up," Mo muttered.

While Mo and Darby bickered, Buzz, still trapped inside his own cone, walked to the door.

"So, we can open the door," he said, pressing the button. The door swished open. "But these things won't let us leave."

Buzz gestured to the red security cone surrounding him. "Sox, can you turn these off?"

Sox batted with his paws, but he had about as much luck as the rest of us.

"I can't reach the controls," he said.

We were running out of ideas fast. I groaned internally. What would Grandma do in a situation like this? I noticed Darby watching the door carefully.

"If one were breaking into a place with a security system, theoretically . . . one would cut the power," she muttered, pressing against the walls of the cone. "If one could."

I wasn't sure what she was talking about, but Mo leaned over to look at a large gray box on the wall.

"Maybe one can," he said, pointing to the box. "That's the Fast Draw Five Hundred power source. Read about it in the Junior Patrol manual. It's also called the Glass Jaw Five Hundred, because if you hit it hard enough, it explodes."

Huh, now there was an idea. I raised my fist and slammed it against the inside edge of the cone. It was solid—solid enough to do some damage.

"We can hit it with this," I announced.

"Wait, with *us*?" Darby shouted.

"Yeah. Section 1.45 of the Junior Patrol handbook: 'A soldier is their own best weapon.'"

"He just said it explodes!" Darby said, pointing at Mo.

"Do you have a better section of the handbook in mind?" I asked.

No one said a word. I was right: there was nothing else in the handbook that worked better in this situation. All those late nights spent studying had really paid off.

"Okay, okay," Buzz said. "I'll open the door, you slam into the power source . . ."

Then he pointed at the cones.

"These things will disappear, and we'll walk right out."

Mo, Darby, and I all agreed. It sounded like

a solid plan. Sox was the only one who seemed uncertain it would work.

"Ready?" Buzz asked. We nodded and Buzz slammed the door button. Together, Mo, Darby, Sox, and I slammed into the gray box. Nothing happened, so we tried again, and again, and again. But it was no use. The four of us weren't enough.

"We're just not heavy enough," I said. "Buzz, we need you."

"Wait, in there?" he asked, incredulous. "But if it doesn't work, I won't be able to save you."

There he went again, talking about saving us instead of working with us. Why couldn't he see what a great team we could be?

"You don't need to save us," I said. "You need to *join* us."

For a moment Buzz considered what I had said. Then he slammed the door button one more time and ran toward us at full speed. When he reached us, his momentum pushed our cone into the power box and it made a loud crack.

Now we were making progress! We backed up and slammed into the box over and over until it began to spark. With a running start, we all shouted, "Again!" and ran at the box once, twice, three more times.

Finally, the box exploded and the cones disappeared. We had done it! But we didn't get a chance to celebrate.

We heard a loud creaky groan. Suddenly, the command center dropped into a slant. It had been built over the crater's cliff, and it sounded like its support beams were giving out.

It was not good.

Not good at all.

"Go! Go!" Buzz shouted, pointing to the door.

We stumbled to our feet and ran for the exit, but when I looked back, I saw Buzz wasn't behind us. He was running toward the console. The coil must have fallen from his pocket and rolled underneath it.

But the room was unstable. Something from the ceiling fell, nearly taking out Mo. I felt panic and I screamed, "Watch out!"

Mo stumbled out of the way, and Buzz grabbed Sox and tossed him back to me as he continued toward the console.

"Buzz! No!" I shouted. It was too dangerous, but Buzz was determined.

"We need the coil!" he shouted back.

Buzz slid underneath the console and grabbed

the coil. He turned back to the door, but the floor snapped in two.

The bad news was the half he stood on was the one falling.

He ran, leapt, and held on to the far edge.

I swallowed hard and rushed toward him as he struggled to keep his grip. As he fell, I lunged forward and grabbed his hand, gritting my teeth. Darby grabbed my other hand, and Mo grabbed hers.

"We got you," I said, my hand clutching his.

We were a chain, using our strength to pull him to safety.

Once he was out of danger, Buzz sat with his legs dangling over the edge of what was left of the command center. Looking at the burning wreckage below, he held up the coil triumphantly.

"I would like . . . if I could . . . just a moment to . . . recuperate, please," he panted.

Honestly, we all needed a break.

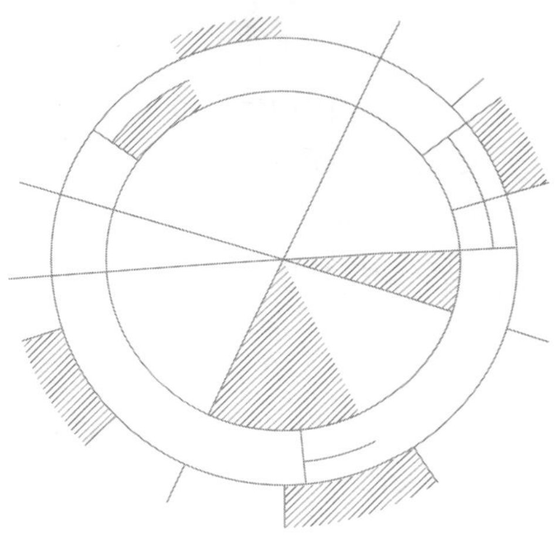

Chapter 15

Behind the command center was an employee break room. Buzz, Darby, and I sat at the tables while Mo brought us packaged sandwiches from a vending machine. I could tell everyone was stunned that Buzz had nearly cliff-dived to an unhappy ending.

I was shaken up, too. I felt like a can of fizzy water.

"Here, eat a little something," Mo said, handing me a sandwich.

Buzz pulled his out of the packaging and looked at it with a confused grimace. "Huh. This is . . . uh . . . What, uh . . . what's . . . what's happening here?"

After taking a chomp out of mine, I asked, "Something wrong with your sandwich?"

"Why is the . . . why is the meat on the outside?" He frowned.

"'Cause it's a sandwich," Mo said, taking a bite out of his.

"No. The bread is supposed to be on the outside," Buzz said.

"What, like bread-meat-bread?" Mo asked, confused.

"Yeah, but this is all . . . wet," Buzz said, looking with disgust at the meat juice dripping off his fingers.

Grandma had told me lots of stories about life on her old planet, but she had never said anything about bread-meat-bread sandwiches. It made me wonder if she was the reason sandwiches had become the way they were now.

"Yeah. Juicy fingers, man. That's the best part," Mo assured him.

I cocked my head. "When's the last time you had a sandwich?"

"I don't know," Buzz said, shrugging. "A hundred years ago? Give or take."

Mo shook his head, chuckling to himself. "This guy . . . Bread-meat-bread . . ."

"It's too much bread. That would just suck all the moisture out of your mouth," Darby said. She and Mo laughed at that.

"Good one, Darby," Mo said, patting her on the back.

Darby's laughing turned into loud choking. I ran over, wrapped my hands around her, and did the Heimlich maneuver until a hunk of soppy sandwich flew out of her mouth and landed in front of Sox.

"You okay?" I asked Darby.

"I'm fine," she replied. "But pen boy doesn't look too good."

A little embarrassed, he looked at all of us. Slumping his shoulders, he said, "I almost killed Darby. I almost got us all killed back there. I can't do anything right."

I went over to him and said, "Hey, listen to me."

He looked at me with sad eyes.

"It was just a mistake. We're allowed to make a mistake every now and then," I assured him, but Mo didn't seem convinced.

So I looked at Buzz for some reinforcement. "Right, Buzz?"

Caught off guard, Buzz looked at me. "Oh—uh . . ."

Then he addressed Mo in an encouraging voice. "Just try to be a little better."

Mo nodded but kept his head hung. Buzz's encouragement helped a little, but Space Rangers were supposed to give the best pep talks, and that hadn't been a very good one.

Buzz didn't notice the you-can-do-better-than-that look I shot at him. All of his attention was on a framed picture of Grandma hanging on the wall. In the picture, she used a gigantic pair of scissors to cut a ribbon at the mining facility's opening ceremony. While Grandma had overseen construction projects all over T'Kani Prime, Buzz had failed mission after mission. And every time he came back, the world became a little less familiar.

After all, years down here were only minutes to him on his light speed spaceship. As I glanced at Grandma's picture, I thought about her patience and understanding for Buzz. Maybe his being resistant to doing things our way was his attempt to hold on to the only life he knew.

"Listen, I just, uh . . . I just . . ." Buzz began

again. "When I first went to the Academy, I wasn't, you know . . . good. I screwed up. Every day. Got tangled in the obstacle course. My hands shook so much I couldn't hit the target. Not the bull's-eye—the *whole* target. And I was going to quit after the first week. I was *not* Space Ranger material."

Mo lifted his head to look at Buzz. His expression was hopeful. "Really?"

"Yeah," Buzz said with a nod, then pointed to me. "But her grandma saw something in me. So I started looking for it, too."

When Mo smiled, I smiled a little, too. My heart swelled with affection for Grandma as Buzz's story reminded me of Rule #2: Always believe in the best of people, even if they don't believe in themselves.

"Grandma always said she believed in you," I told Buzz.

Buzz winced like he was in pain. "Yeah. She believed I could fix this mistake I made. And that belief cost her everything."

The mistake he had made? Grandma had never said it was Buzz's mistake that got them stuck on T'Kani. She always talked about crash-landing and what they did next, but she never blamed Buzz for any of it. Was this why he was so stubborn about doing this mission on his own?

He was being so hard on himself. He obviously didn't know how much Grandma had loved her life on T'Kani Prime—how much she loved all of us.

"Everything?" I repeated, not believing that one bit. "No. She had Grandma Kiko, my dad, me, all her friends. She had a whole life on this planet, Buzz. All of us have . . . except for you."

"Yeah, but we wanted to be Space Rangers again. We wanted to matter," he said.

I looked at him like he was a ridiculous bread-meat-bread sandwich. "Oh, believe me. She mattered."

Buzz fell quiet and thoughtfully looked back at the framed photo of Grandma, taking a bite of his sandwich. He went *huh* and studied it, smiling a little.

"It is pretty good this way," he admitted, chewing.

"Yeah. Bread-meat-bread." I snorted. "How long did you do it like that?"

While Buzz chewed, he thought about it, then said, "Forever."

Hmm, maybe he was starting to see there were

other ways to do things. Like letting us help. Buzz looked at us all one more time before standing.

"Come on. Let's go put this part in the ship. Then I'll drop you guys off before I finish the mission," Buzz said.

Never mind. It sounded like Buzz was still determined to fix his mistake on his own, but he needed us. I just knew it. We could stop the Zurg ship and its robots, but we had to do it together as a team. When everyone had given up on Buzz, Grandma hadn't.

And we wouldn't, either.

Buzz just didn't know it yet.

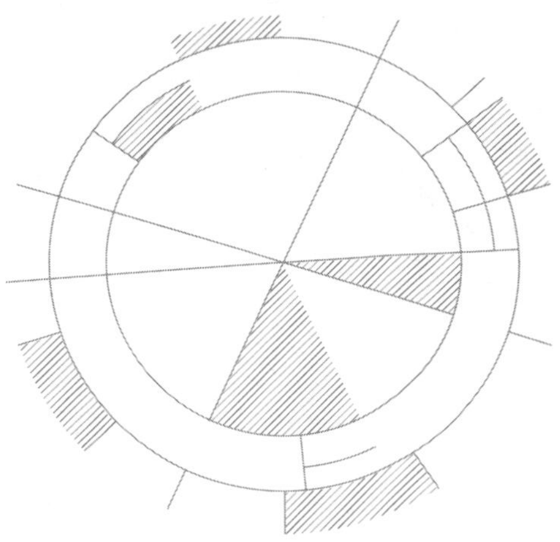

Chapter 16

Buzz opened the break room's door and stuck his head out, checking to make sure the coast was clear. Then he motioned to everyone that it was okay to leave. Sox led us down a tunnel and outside into the cold dark.

We ended up at the bottom of the mine's enormous crater. I felt like a tiny bug, and the black sky looked like a lid trying to keep me trapped down here.

I gulped hard, not daring to peer up.

"The ship is this way," Sox said, guiding us toward it.

"What? Are you going to do the whole mission alone?" I asked, but I already knew his answer.

"I can do it," Buzz assured me.

"Because you got a Hawthorne right here, ready to unleash the legacy of her family name!" I reasoned.

Buzz glanced at me as he walked. "Izzy, I spent years doing that—trying to be just like your grandma. You know what she finally told me? She said, 'Lightyear, one day you're gonna come up against something you don't think you can do. And from then on, you're you.' "

Then he kept walking.

"But what if being me . . ." I trailed off, looking back at Mo and Darby. Afraid they'd hear me, I whispered, "Isn't enough?"

"You'll never know until you put it to the test," Buzz said.

A loud explosion suddenly knocked us off our feet. A massive hole had been blown into a wall of the mine.

I heard Mo coughing and others groaning.

I struggled to get to my feet with a grunt.

The rocky ground shook beneath us. Then a robot marched through the new hole with heavy stomps. But this robot wasn't anything like the zyclopes. It was purple and huge, twice the size of the others. The robot loomed over us with its two glowing red eyes and a large yellow mouth.

We were in big trouble.

Again.

Buzz gasped, then commanded roughly, "Run!"

We all scrambled to our feet and dashed away from the evil-looking robot, but in my peripheral vision, I saw Mo trip over Sox and bump into Darby, causing all three of them to tumble to the ground in a heap.

I skidded to a stop and rushed back to them to make sure they were all right.

I gawked as the menacing robot stomped up to us.

"No!" Buzz shouted.

I thought it would use its feet to squish us like bugs, but its long legs stepped right over us.

"It's after me!" Buzz yelled. "Go back to the ship."

"But—but, Buzz!" I shouted back as the robot pursued him.

"Go!" Buzz demanded before he pivoted, ran fast, and bravely jumped down a canyon. I clenched my jaw as I looked toward the Armadillo. An idea stormed into my head. Determination fired me up to act on it.

In the tangled pile, Darby sighed. "We're not going to the ship, are we?"

"Nope," I said. "No pilot, no flying outta here!"

"Excellent point, Izzy!" Sox concurred, shaking pebbles off himself.

We rushed to the canyon's edge and watched the giant robot chase Buzz through an obstacle course of debris and boulders before he raced back into the mine.

I narrowed my eyes and addressed the group. "I think I know where he's going. Everyone, follow me. We're going to stop that giant purple robot in its tracks. Darby, have you ever operated a plasma drill?"

"No, but I've always wanted to," Darby replied with a wide grin. Without waiting for more instructions, she broke into a run, leaping over the ledge. The rest of us followed suit, jumping levels carved out by the mining operation's machines, and ran straight into a nearby tunnel.

Our boots pounded on the rough rock floors and echoed.

"Faster, team!" I ordered, hoping we could get to the intended destination before Buzz and the robot did. At the end of the tunnel, we found a dormant plasma drill.

"Perfect," I panted, then turned to Darby. "Darby, I need you to do what you do best."

As I pointed to the heavy piece of machinery, she smiled and pulled out her space lockpick.

"Thought you'd never ask," she said, cracking her knuckles. Within seconds, she undid the lock to the plasma drill's door. All four of us climbed inside, and Darby sat in the operator's seat, because of course Darby knew how to operate a plasma drill. She never stopped surprising me with her hidden skills. It was just the sort of thing I knew Buzz would learn to appreciate about our team.

"They're coming," I whispered as I heard and felt the robot's heavy footsteps. We saw Buzz squeeze through a narrow space between two massive piles of rocks, but the robot smashed through them easily. There was nowhere else for Buzz to run as the robot backed him into a wall right beside us.

"Darby," I whispered worriedly.

"Nearly ready," she assured me, flipping switches, pulling levers, and pressing buttons.

"Do you really know how to work this thing?" Mo asked, crossing his arms.

Darby shot him a glare. "It's as easy as riding a hoverbike."

"I don't know how to ride a hoverbike," Mo said.

Darby rolled her eyes. "That doesn't surprise me one bit."

While they bickered, I saw the robot's metal claws reach out to Buzz.

"Darby, do it now. Now, now, now, please," I said urgently.

"Now? You got it," she said, taking hold of the control stick to make the plasma drill lift up Buzz.

"Blast it?" she asked, holding her finger over a big round button.

"Blast it," I confirmed with a nod. She smashed the button, and the plasma laser charged up and blasted the robot's broad chest. It collapsed backward, knocked out cold.

Buzz looked at us through the windshield in surprise.

"This is definitely a violation of my parole," Darby said with a chuckle, using the controls to turn the drill toward the wall behind us. She pressed the blast button again and made a new hole for us to escape through.

"C'mon! Let's get out of here!" I said, jumping out of the cockpit.

Everyone followed my lead.

We climbed through the hole, not daring to look back. We exited the tunnel and slid down a rocky hillside to get to the Armadillo. Suddenly, metal pods rained down from the skies, crashing to the snowy ground.

We hurried into the Armadillo and buckled up.

"Ready yourselves for launch!" Buzz said, looking back at us from his spot in the pilot's chair. "Operation Surprise Party is back on!"

I gaped. Was Buzz saying what I thought he was saying? "What? With us?"

Buzz nodded. "What? Am I going to do the whole mission alone?"

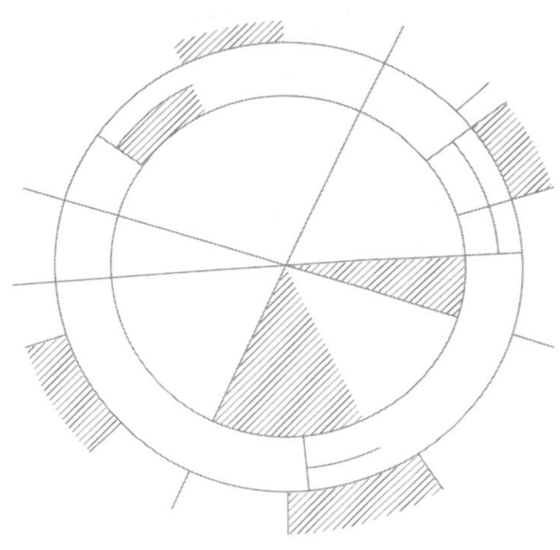

Chapter 17

"We can't launch yet. I still need five minutes to make the repair," Sox reminded us as the zyclopes burst from their metal pods.

"We can't sit here for five minutes!" Darby shouted, throwing up her hands.

"The ship still has hover capabilities," Sox informed her.

Well, that was definitely better than nothing.

"Then let's use them," Buzz said as he fired up the Armadillo. It floated up and hovered above the ground. He gave it throttle, and the ship raced off. As the pods continued to fall out of the sky, Buzz swerved left and right to dodge them.

It didn't help matters that the zyclopes chased after us, too, using powerful jets on their feet to fly.

Sox's tail stuck out from underneath the dashboard as he worked on repairs.

"Repair ten percent complete," he announced, which meant we needed more time.

An idea skipped into my head.

"We might lose them in the fire geysers," I said urgently.

"Point the way," Buzz said to me.

In the copilot seat, I nodded, ready to give him directions.

Buzz looked back at Mo and Darby. "You two, blast some robots."

With permission from Buzz, Darby smiled, not hesitating to open the weapons case. Because we were the Junior Patrol, we weren't finished with our munitions training yet, but it probably wasn't best to tell Buzz that.

"What? What are *you* going to do?" Mo asked worriedly.

Darby picked up a bazooka and propped it on her shoulder. "I'm gonna dance with Mr. Boom."

As I gave Buzz directions, I looked over my

shoulder to see Darby move to the back door of the ship. She kicked it open with her boot, and a robot tried to get inside, but she quickly fired her weapon and blasted the robot.

"Now that's satisfying," she said.

Darby split open the bazooka, ejecting a hot-hot-hot empty shell.

"Twenty percent complete!" Sox called out from underneath the dashboard near my feet.

"Out of a hundred?" Mo asked, panicking.

Buzz jerked the yoke left and right, steering through the obstacle course of pods and flying robots.

As more robot pods fell from the darkened skies, the zyclopes sped toward the Armadillo.

"They're gaining on us! Where are those fire geysers?" Buzz asked, determined.

I pointed to the geysers on the horizon. "Dead ahead! Don't worry. I know every last inch of it."

Then I gave him a confident nod, pointing to my nameplate.

A zyclops managed to get closer to the Armadillo, plucked the transport disk from its chest, and held it out to slap it on. *Oh, no!*

Here are two things you needed to know about the fire geysers:

1) The fire geysers made lots of steam, which made it very hard to see.

2) Lots of steam plus no sun was a very bad combo.

As the Armadillo hover-raced through the thick cover, a suspicious dark blob took shape ahead of us. *Could that be a—*

I widened my eyes.

"Watch out!" I shouted, pointing at a gigantic stalagmite.

But it was too late.

I gritted my teeth and winced as the Armadillo clipped the stalagmite. When the rock slammed into the zyclops robot and its transport disk, our threat teleported away in an eyeblink.

Checking over my shoulder to make sure the rest of the gang was okay, I saw Darby handing a grenade to Mo.

"Throw this," Darby instructed.

"Okay, but hold on! Let's just—" Mo started, nervous.

Darby interrupted him, pulling the grenade's pin. "Throw it!"

In a panic, Mo chucked it out the back at two robots, destroying their legs. The two half robots leaned into each other for support, and their transport disks bumped, making them disappear.

I faced the front again as Buzz steered the ship into the fire geysers, a stretch of land with craters and bubbling pools of molten lava.

"Fire geysers dead ahead!" I announced, clocking familiar landmarks.

"Here we go!" Buzz shouted, sounding determined and ready.

He skillfully maneuvered the Armadillo through the geysers.

From underneath the dashboard, Sox announced, "Fifty percent complete."

Just then, a geyser shot fire into the air. Buzz swerved around it sharply, but the ship's underbelly dragged on the rough, rocky ground. I cringed at the sound of rock scraping against metal. A box of shells tipped over, and they clanked and rolled around the ship's floor.

"Hey, we have explosives back here!" Darby shouted grumpily at our pilot.

As I saw the telltale signs of a fire geyser ready to explode, I shouted, "Left!"

Buzz turned the yoke to the left hard as the fire geyser spat out its column of flame. Everyone and everything inside the Armadillo tilted sideways. Well, everyone except Sox. He was latched to whatever was under the ship's dashboard, still working diligently.

I looked out the window, craning my neck to see a robot that had been chasing us collide with the flames and burn up. I had no time to do a happy dance as I heard a heavy thunk against the ship's hull, which meant another zyclops and its transport disk had caught up to us.

Buzz must've heard it, too, because he steered us to the right before the robot could press the teleport button.

"Give me something!" Buzz ordered, reaching his arm into the back. Darby attached a white gauntlet with a shiny red button to his arm.

"Here!" she said.

Buzz took his arm back, aimed his gauntlet at the robot, and shot a blast. The robot careened into four other robots, and all five teleported away, leaving only one more zyclops to chase us across the fire geysers.

I stared in sheer awe at the awesomeness I had just witnessed. Had Buzz taken a perfect shot at a moving target while piloting an Armadillo through the fire geysers? Yes. Yes, he had!

As Sox continued to work on repairs, he announced, "Ninety percent complete!"

"Izzy, do you know how to transfer power on the fly?" Buzz asked me.

"I've read about it," I answered. A week ago, I'd fallen asleep studying, using manuals for my pillows. I'd dreamed about piloting a ship. Now was my chance to prove I could do it wide awake.

Buzz flipped a few switches. "Well, it's about to get real."

At the back, Darby loaded up Mr. Boom with another shell.

"Do you need my help with anything?" Mo asked.

"Absolutely not," Darby said, propping Mr. Boom on her shoulder again.

"Ninety-five percent complete," Sox announced.

"Ready thrusters!" Buzz instructed me.

I found the button and pushed it, shouting out, "Done!"

Darby walked to the Armadillo's opened back door and lined up a shot at the robot, but it was swerving back and forth to avoid ending up a pile of smoldering rubbish like the rest of its buddies.

"Remember from training . . . you don't pull the trigger. You *squeeze* the trigger," Mo reminded her.

Darby looked at him, annoyed. "Are *you* telling *me* how to do this?"

"Ninety-nine percent complete!" Sox said, his tail wagging underneath the console.

"Transfer to—" Buzz began.

At the same time, we shouted, "Oscillating power."

I found another button and pushed it, too. "Done!"

Sox popped his head out from underneath the dash. "One hundred percent complete!"

Buzz looked at a glowing gauge on the dashboard that showed the fuel cell's readiness.

"Okay! Ready to launch once the fuel cell is—" Buzz started.

"Ready, launch!" I finished for him.

"Secure," he finished for himself at the same time, but it was too late. I had already pressed the launch button, accidentally ejecting the fuel crystal. The now fuel-less Armadillo slammed into the ground.

The collision threw Darby off balance as she fired a rocket at the final robot, and it dodged the attack easily. We jumped and bumped in our spots as the Armadillo ground to a complete stop.

I looked at Buzz in horror at what I done.

"Oh, no," I gasped. My heart sank like a rock, not only at my mistake but at the fact that my mistake had let Buzz down.

He looked through the window, spotting the fuel cell on the ground just beyond the ship.

"Blast!" he growled, running out of the Armadillo to face the incoming robot.

"Grab the crystal!" he ordered me, trying to keep the robot at bay by aiming his arm blaster and firing. The blast hit the robot, destroying its arm. But that didn't stop the robot from racing toward the canister holding the crystal, just as I was.

I ran as fast as I could, stretching my arm out for it as soon as it was within reach, but the robot snatched it up first and disappeared with the help of its transport disk.

I stood there in shock, staring at the spot the robot had teleported from.

Buzz fell to his knees, stunned. "No."

The icy wind blew through the fire geysers, and my heart broke at the fact that my failure had led us to this moment.

My eyes moved over to a speechless Darby and Mo.

Did they think I was a failure, too?

"I—" The words stopped in my throat as I hesitantly walked to Buzz and stood over him. Seeing him so hopeless and dejected, knowing he was this way because of me, made my stomach twist.

The fuel cell was gone *because of me*.

"Buzz? I'm so sorry. Everything was happening so fast, and I—I just—I thought I had it, and . . ." I said, fumbling over my words. "I made a mistake."

Buzz looked up at me, utterly defeated.

"Yeah," he sighed sadly. "Welcome to the club."

I hung my head, guilt washing over me.

"Your mistake wouldn't even matter if I hadn't made mine. Years ago," Buzz said.

"Okay, but we're not done, right? We can still do something!" I said hopefully.

"Izzy! Look around," Buzz said, getting to his feet. He gestured to our surroundings. "There is nothing to do. The mission . . . is over."

I opened my mouth to say something, but this was the first time I didn't know what to say or how to help.

Buzz walked away from me—away from all of us—in sad frustration.

I took a step forward, worried. "Where are you going?"

Buzz didn't answer me. He just kept walking. The distance between us grew bigger and bigger. Suddenly, a bad feeling shot through me. Something was wrong, but I didn't know what.

"Buzz!" I called out his name warningly.

"I just need to be . . . by myself," Buzz said sadly, refusing to look back at me.

Just then, a clawed robotic hand snatched Buzz up. Buzz yelped, struggling to get out.

We all rushed toward him to help—to fight.

"No!" I screamed, my boots pounding on the ground as I raced toward him.

The hand retreated into the extended arm of a robot sporting a cruel yellow frown. The big purple robot emerged from the steam-fog and held Buzz up, examining him with its glowing red eyes. It was the robot we had blasted with the plasma drill!

I ran faster as it looked at us, reaching for the transport disk on its chest.

"What? How did you—" Buzz's distressed words were cut off as the robot pressed a button, making them both disappear.

"Buzz!" I screamed at the top of my lungs.

My voice echoed across the fire geysers.

IZZY AND GRANDMA'S BLAST FROM THE PAST

Control Tower

At school, we made space-jet models for a science experiment to learn about the principles of flight: lift, gravity, thrust, and drag. We designed them on our school tablets, and a 3D printer reproduced them. Mr. Cloud said the best way to learn knowledge was to apply knowledge, so he told us to get our space jets and lined us up to go outside.

He drew a line in the mud far away, and we stood in a straight row.

"All right, let's see which model goes the farthest," Mr. Cloud said. Then he counted down from ten, and we threw our space-jet models. Some nose-dived into the mud right away, some spun and knocked into others, and some flew straight.

Mine flew straight and soared past the line in the mud.

"Very good, Izzy," Mr. Cloud said, picking up my space jet. "How did you build such a good model?"

"From my dad's flight simulator games," I answered proudly. The ones I played let me design all kinds of spaceships to outrun enemy ships. I knew all the names of all the parts and why each of them was super important. "And my grandma told me all about the ships she used to fly when she was a Space Ranger. She takes me all over T'Kani Prime to see the ships and the outposts and everything."

He handed me back my space jet, and we practiced flying them some more.

At dismissal, some of my classmates came up to my desk.

"Where is your grandma taking you next, Izzy?" Serenity asked, excitement making her eyes sparkly.

During lunchtime, they'd always gobble down their food and listen to me tell stories about all the places Grandma had taken me. Kids weren't allowed to leave the base, because T'Kani Prime had lots of dangers, and some buildings on base weren't safe for kids, either. But because Grandma was the commander, I could go places other kids couldn't.

"We're going to the Control Tower today," I said excitedly, stuffing my school things into my backpack. But I kept my space jet out, because I wanted to show Grandma.

"That's so cool!" Wyatt said, bouncing on his feet.

"You're so lucky!" Eli said with a big grin, one of his front teeth missing.

"Wow, I'm jealous!" Stella said, pouting. They followed me out of the classroom and into the corridor, begging me to tell them everything at lunch tomorrow. I promised them I would and ran to Grandma.

"Look, Grandma, look," I said, showing her my space-jet model. "We did flight experiments, and mine flew the farthest."

She took my space jet and examined it carefully, her smile growing. "Very impressive, sweetheart. It's fit for a Space Ranger to pilot."

I gasped excitedly, jumping up and down. "Really, Grandma? You really think so?"

"I know so, Izzy. I used to be a Space Ranger," Grandma said, giving me a wink.

We took a motor kart-truck to the Control Tower. It was *way* on the other side of the base, by the airstrip, far away from school and home to keep everyone safe during spaceship launches and landings. We rode past all kinds of buildings and other places in the restricted areas.

"That's the silo," I said, pointing to the pyramid-shaped building.

"Oh, and that's the launchpad," I gasped loudly, clapping my hands.

The motor kart driver dropped us off at a tall building with a satellite dish and a big antenna at the very top.

"This is the Control Tower, Izzy. Those who work in here are called controllers. A controller's job is to make sure the pilot launches and lands safely and doesn't get lost," Grandma said, taking my hand. We went inside and rode an elevator all the way to the top floor. The empty room we walked into had glass windows all around it. Just like at Mission Control, there were computers everywhere.

"Whoa," I said, looking all around.

"I used to work here," Grandma said, but she sounded sad. "I loved watching spaceships rocket into space and come back home safely."

She walked me over to the windows and pointed out to the airstrip.

"That's where Buzz is going to land after he finishes his mission," she said. All the other places Grandma took me to had lots and lots of people doing their jobs, but the Control Tower had no one.

"Grandma, where is everyone?" I asked. "Are they on a lunch break?"

Grandma laughed softly, shaking her head. "No, sweetheart. They aren't on a lunch break.

It's empty because there hasn't been a spaceship launch or landing in a very long time."

"Shouldn't they be waiting for Buzz?" I asked, frowning. Grandma's friend was up in space, trying to help us.

"In the beginning they did," Grandma said. "But some got tired of waiting, dear."

"Are you tired of waiting, Grandma?" I asked.

"No, Izzy. Never. Sometimes I come here, look at the sky, and wait," Grandma said, and her face became sadder and sadder. "Because someone has to wait for him. It's the least I can do for him, since he's done and sacrificed so much for us."

I let go of Grandma's hand and gave her a hug.

"Don't be sad, Grandma. I'll wait for him, too," I said.

I heard Grandma sniffle, and I looked up to see tears in her eyes, but they didn't fall down.

"That makes me so happy, Izzy," she said with a smile, hugging me back. Then she turned on the computers to show me how they worked. I even got to wear a controller headset, but it messed up my hair puffs. So Grandma fixed my hairdo for me.

When it was time to leave, me and Grandma climbed back into the motor kart. I picked up my space jet again, picturing myself as a Space Ranger inside it. In my imagination, Grandma was in the Control Tower, talking through my cockpit's radio.

"Captain Izzy, prepare for landing," Grandma said.

"Copy that," I said, flipping switches and pressing buttons like a real pilot. "Prepare for landing!"

My imagination flew away when Grandma said my name.

"I know a place where you can fly your space jet," she said, winking at me. "Would you like to go?"

I nodded excitedly, and Grandma asked the driver to take us to the airstrip!

When we got there, I hopped out and skipped to the dotted line running down the middle of the very long runway. Grandma came up to me from behind and put her hands on my shoulders.

"All right, cadet. Show me how well your ship flies," she said encouragingly.

"Roger that, Commander," I said, squinting one eye to get the right aim. Then I threw my space-jet model. It flew straight, like back at school, but a wind blew, making it go farther and higher.

Grandma squeezed my shoulders gently.

"I think you'll make a fine pilot," she said.

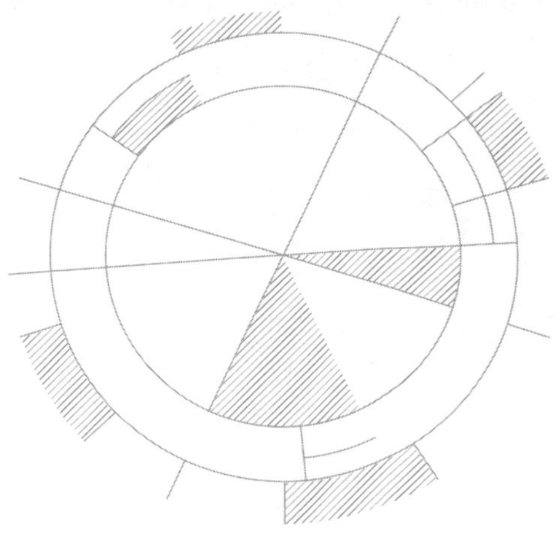

Chapter 18

Underneath the dark skies, the four of us stood still. A fire geyser nearby erupted, spewing lava and steam high up into the air. I felt like a fire geyser ready to explode. Disappointment and guilt bubbled and gurgled in me like red-hot lava.

Because of me, the fuel cell had ejected.

Because of me, the Armadillo had crashed.

Because of me, Darby hadn't been able to line up a shot at the robot.

Because of me, that evil purple robot had kidnapped Buzz.

Ever since I was little, all I had ever wanted was to be a Space Ranger—to continue the Hawthorne legacy. I studied hard and trained even harder. I followed Grandma's three rules like they were a part of the Star Command Code.

Now, as I wore her Space Ranger suit, I didn't feel like one. Wearing it was no different from dressing up in one made of cardboard. All this time, I had been playing pretend. The nameplate on my chest had my last name on it, but I felt like I'd spent my whole life just pretending to be a Hawthorne. Grandma was an absolute legend at everything she did. How could I ever be as good as her when I wasn't even good at being me?

I stared at the spot the robot and Buzz had teleported from.

"I messed this all up!" I growled out. Tears stung my eyes, but I held them back as best I could.

"It was just a mistake," Mo said encouragingly, stepping closer to me. "Remember what you told me?"

Yeah, I remembered what I had told him in the break room: *It was just a mistake. We're allowed to make a mistake every now and then.*

I shook my head, clenching my hands into fists. "This one's different."

Darby frowned, asking, "Why?"

As I squeezed my hands, anger bubbled in my voice like lava in a fire geyser. "Because it's *mine*!

I'm supposed to be as good as my grandma. I'm supposed to be a Hawthorne."

I ripped the nameplate off my suit and let it fall from my hand. I didn't deserve to wear it or Grandma's Space Ranger suit.

"But I'm not," I said sadly.

Goose bumps covered my skin as the enemy Zurg ship sailed across the sky and right into space, taking Buzz with it. I whispered his name worriedly.

Sox followed me as I marched to the other side of the Armadillo to examine the empty fuel cell compartment. To confront my grave mistake. To come face to face with my failure.

If Grandma had been there, how would she have reacted? I didn't even have enough courage to imagine how she'd look at me or what she'd say. Grandma had spent decades on T'Kani Prime waiting for Buzz to come back safely from his missions, and now I, *her granddaughter*, was the reason he was in danger.

Darby pointed at the Armadillo, looking at Sox. "Hey, cat, do you know how to fly this thing?" Darby asked.

"There's no fuel," Sox reminded her.

"See, this is why we should have never gotten

in over our heads!" Mo complained, throwing his hands up.

"What did you want to do? Wait at the outpost until the robots found us?" Darby asked, crossing her arms and sounding annoyed.

"That's better than being stranded out here where no one's *ever* gonna find us!" Mo shot back.

"Ugh. You are the last person I want to be stuck with in a life-and-death situation," Darby groaned.

"Well, you're in luck. Because this is just a death situation!" Mo barked.

There had to be something we could do, but my mind kept drawing blanks. Without a fuel crystal, the Armadillo couldn't even turn on. Without a pilot, we couldn't fly it. And without either of those, Buzz drifted farther and farther away from us.

As I continued to examine the fuel panel, Sox's ears started to spin as if he had detected something. He was, after all, Buzz's robotic feline companion. He was our only connection to Buzz. I looked at him, hopeful.

But when his ears drooped sadly, my heart did, too.

"I've completely lost Buzz. He's too far away now to track," Sox informed me. The news made me feel angry, frustrated, and . . . hopeless.

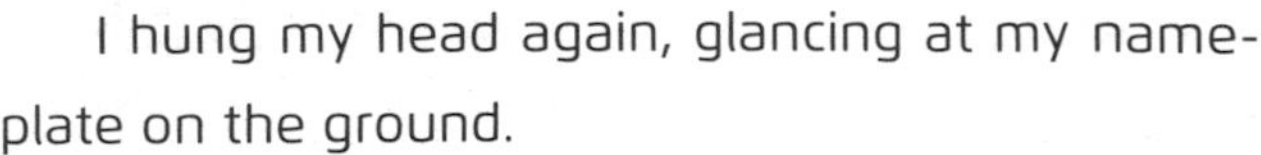

I hung my head again, glancing at my nameplate on the ground.

I'm sorry, Grandma.

Sox rubbed against my legs, trying to make me feel better.

But we had to face it: we had a perfectly good ship, and we couldn't even—

My thoughts came to a grinding halt and my eyes stretched wide as I noticed something stuck to the ship.

No, it can't be. Can it?

Oh, oh, oh! It is!

An idea soared into my head. It was an idea Grandma would approve of wholeheartedly.

"Everyone! Inside!" I ordered, running to the ship's opposite side, where the door was wide open. Sox followed suit, galloping on his furry paws.

Darby looked at me, confused. "What?"

"Get inside the ship!" I repeated, gesturing for Mo and Darby to come along as I climbed back inside the Armadillo.

After everyone got in and the door was shut, Mo panted out, "What's after us now?"

Darby glanced around the back of the ship in a panic. "We don't have any more weapons!"

"That's okay! I have a plan," I promised, plopping into the pilot's seat—Buzz's seat.

"I'm only borrowing it for a little while," I whispered softly to Buzz, as if he were here with me—with us—and not a captive on a Zurg ship filled with an army of robots.

Sox hopped into the copilot seat and asked, "Where are we going?"

I leaned far out the window and clocked the transport disk stuck to the side of the Armadillo. Earlier, when the zyclopes chased us across the fire geysers, one of them had slapped on that disk to kidnap us all and take us back to its Zurg ship.

I gulped at the sight of it, but a conversation I'd had long ago came back to me:

"You know what I think the B *in plan B stands for?" Grandma asked. "Bravery, because when plan A didn't work, you didn't give up. You tried something else."*

I steeled my nerves and told the team my plan B.

"We're going to space."

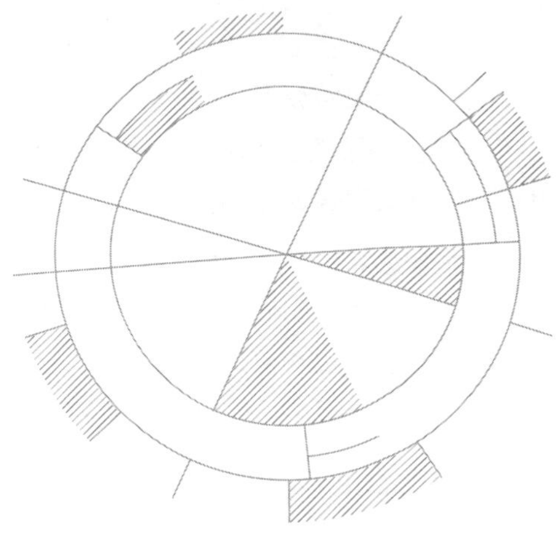

Chapter 19

I squeezed my eyes shut and did the breathing exercises Grandma had taught me when I was little. *I can do this. I can do this. I can do this.* I balled my hand into a fist and slammed it down against the transport disk, teleporting us and the Armadillo off T'Kani Prime's Dark Side. Within an eyeblink, we had arrived in the Zurg ship's teleportation bay. It worked! I was in space!

Oh, no, I was in space.

My fears tried to creep in on me like a swarm of bugs, but I squashed them deep inside of me. In order to save Buzz and everyone back on T'Kani Prime, I couldn't let my phobia bully me.

But it was also totally okay to freak out, because I WAS IN SPACE!

"Operation Surprise Party, here we go!" I declared, putting on a brave face for the team as we all climbed out of the Armadillo.

"Hup-hup!" Darby and Mo voiced jointly.

"Hup-hup!" I joined in.

As I looked around the spacious teleportation bay, more of Grandma's words came back to me: *A Space Ranger must map out their surroundings.*

We and the Armadillo stood on a platform. There weren't any yellow or purple robots around, but I feared if we didn't hurry, we'd have company soon.

"We need to protect our escape ship," I said, pointing at the Armadillo.

Then I clocked a long corridor and pointed an accusatory finger at it.

"If any robots are going to stop us, they'll come through that door," I said.

Darby gestured to herself and Mo. "Don't worry. We'll seal it off."

"You go find Buzz," Mo said to me.

"I'll track the chip in his dog tags," Sox chimed in, his ears spinning for a signal. Confused, he turned his head in one direction, then another.

I frowned, stepping a little closer to him.

"What's wrong?" I asked worriedly.

"I'm getting a double signal," Sox said. "I'll triangulate. That'll get us close enough. Come on!"

Then he sprang away in the other direction, galloping across the teleportation bay. I raced after him, but not before grabbing a magnetic transport disk from a wall dispenser and slapping it onto my back.

"A shortcut back to this spot!" I yelled to Mo and Darby, hoping they'd each grab one for themselves. If we were all equipped with one, all we would have to do was hit it, and it would take us right back to the Armadillo.

As Sox and I ran to the pentagon-shaped door, I also yelled back to them, "I believe in you guys!"

"We believe in you, too!" Mo and Darby shouted back at me.

"Meow, meow, meow, meow, meow," Sox chanted as he followed Buzz's signal, leading me down a maze of corridors.

Then he said excitedly, "Oh! The signal is tighter now. He has to be straight this way!"

I followed Sox into a room and instantly regretted it. Through the windows was my greatest archnemesis of all:

Space.

Endless, endless darker-than-dark outer space.

Immediately, I looked to the floor, my phobia knotting up my stomach.

"Bguhh, okay. Sp—that's a lot of space," I stuttered out, then closed my eyes to give myself a much-needed pep talk. "Keep it together, keep it together. . . ."

My eyes snapped open and I jumped at the sudden sound of blaring alarms.

The pentagon-shaped door behind us slid shut.

"Security breach. All areas restricted," a voice announced from an intercom above, which must have meant something had happened with Darby and Mo.

"No!" I screamed, darting to the door.

I banged on it with all my might.

Sox looked around the room, confused.

"I don't understand. The signal says Buzz is fifty meters away," he said.

Hearing Buzz's name reminded me of our mission—my mission.

I looked around, then out the windows.

Geez Louise, that's a whole lotta space.

Finally, I spotted the Zurg ship's bridge, where

Buzz was struggling to get out of the robot's tight clutches. My eyes popped with surprise.

Pointing at them, I gasped, "He's over there."

The robot threw Buzz across the bridge, and I flinched as he smashed into the control panel. But he bounced off it, floating up—as did the robot. The room's artificial gravity must have been switched off.

I turned to Sox, determined. "How do we get over there?"

Sox peered at a different door I hadn't noticed until then.

"Through the air lock," he informed me.

I went to it and pressed my face against its glass, hoping to see another corridor that connected this room with the Zurg ship's command bridge.

But all I saw was—

Gaping, I exclaimed, "Through *there*? There's *nothing* out there!"

Nothing but space and—oh, yeah—MORE SPACE!

"Oh, exactly. Nothing in your way. You just go straight across," Sox said plainly, as if it were the easiest task in the entire universe. All the adventures we'd had down on T'Kani Prime must have short-circuited some of his wires if he thought I'd go through with his plan.

I stared at him in disbelief and yelled, "No!"

Looking back through the window, I watched as a floating Buzz tried to grab the crystal. I grimaced as the robot knocked him out of the way. Quickly, Buzz fired his blaster, striking the robot's reaching hand.

The force of the blaster thrust Buzz backward, flinging him against a window.

I spoke into my wrist communicator, hoping he could hear me.

"Buzz? Buzz!"

I could see him searching for me, but he looked confused.

"Are you okay?" I asked.

Then he turned and spotted me across the ocean of nothingness. He spoke into his wrist communicator.

"No, I—I need help," he admitted tiredly.

Did he know who he was asking for help? It was *my* mistake that had led to the fuel cell's being stolen and his getting kidnapped. That collision against the window must've scrambled up his brain.

I was only good at making things worse.

"Buzz, I'm not my grandma," I sighed, my shoulders drooping. All these years, I'd only ever wanted to prove I was worthy of the Hawthorne family name and Grandma's legacy as one of the greatest Space Rangers in history, but with all my failures and fears, how could I?

I was the reason he was in danger.

He shook his head as if to get rid of all his confusion. Then he looked at me again, realizing it was *me*, Izzy Hawthorne.

"Izzy, I don't need your grandma. I need you."

I stared across the great expanse of space as his words settled in my brain. Buzz needed *me*, Izzy Hawthorne. The Space Ranger who never wanted anyone's help said he needed my help. Not grandma's or anyone else's—mine.

I took a deep breath and looked over at the air lock as an idea brewed in my head. It was the kind of idea you considered as your last resort. If there was any time for an idea like that, it was now.

With the press of a button, the door to the air lock opened. Sox followed me inside the small room.

After the door closed, I knew there was no turning back. Performing my breathing exercises, I pulled my suit's snood over my hair and deployed my helmet, the curved glass clamping into place over my face. Sox hopped up, and the magnets in his pink paw pads stuck to my back like glue.

I continued to *breathe in* and *breathe out*.

You can do this, Izzy Hawthorne. You can do this, because if you can't, you'll be lost in outer space for all eternity. Wait. I squeezed my eyes shut. *Don't think that. If you can't do it, you can't save Buzz.*

Better, but still a bad pep talk.

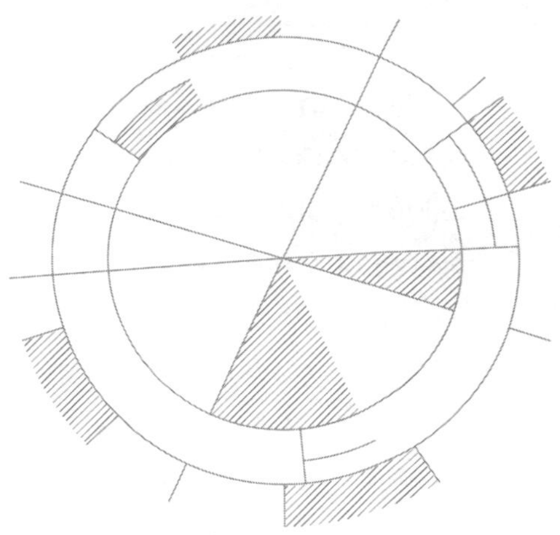

Chapter 20

I stepped up to the air lock's final door and pressed a button to open it. The vast emptiness of space overwhelmed me. I trembled from head to toe as I stood at the air lock's edge and looked out at the blackness. I forgot how to breathe, and I felt dizzy. But then I remembered Grandma's breathing exercises and did a few more, trying to fight the urge to run away.

"Just don't look down," Sox advised. It sounded like good advice until I dared to look up. My heart sank into my stomach as I saw more outer-spacey blackness.

"Or up," he added. "It's all space. It's everywhere. All around you."

That didn't help me at all.

"I'm sorry. I'm probably not helping," he continued, as if he could sense my panic. "Just . . . just go straight. Once you push off, that's the direction you'll go."

I gulped, looking at the bridge room's air lock. "But what if I miss?"

Deep breath in, deep breath out.

"Don't miss," Sox said.

Deep breath in, deep breath out.

"Here I go, Grandma," I announced softly, then took one final deep breath before I jumped into the thing I feared most. As my boots left the air lock's solid floor, I yelped aloud, floating through nothing with outstretched arms.

Ahead of us, through the bridge's windows, the float battle between Buzz and the robot raged on. The robot threw a metal chunk at Buzz to prevent him from reaching the crystal, but Buzz dodged the attack with a nimble spin.

Instead, the metal smacked into the control panel, causing the whole Zurg ship to shift suddenly.

"What?" I yelled, flapping my arms. "Ah, no, no, no, no, NO!"

Panic surged through me as the ship drifted out of my course. I reached up to grab on to something—anything—before I floated away. I felt relief as I grabbed on to a metal bar, but my body swung up, slamming hard into the ship's underside.

It knocked the wind out of me. I panted, gasped, and yelped, struggling to keep a hold of the ship, not realizing that Sox had been knocked off my back.

"Whoa!" he shouted.

"Sox!" I yelled, seeing him drift away.

"Whoa, whoa!" he yelped in terror, falling backward. His round green eyes grew bigger. I stretched out my arm as far as it could go, catching him by the tail. I sighed, my body sagging in relief.

Sox swirled his head around 180 degrees to look back at me.

"Thank you, Izzy," he said.

For a few moments, I stayed still, with one hand on the ship and the other gripping Sox's tail. But I knew we couldn't stay like this forever. Buzz needed us. Slowly, I float-crawled from underneath the ship, scaling up and up until we reached the bridge's air lock. It opened for us, and I panted heavily as we climbed inside.

As the air lock's door closed, the artificial gravity kicked in. No longer weightless, my boots went *thunk* on the floor. My body shook inside Grandma's Space Ranger suit and my heartbeat raced so fast it boomed loudly in my ears.

Seconds before, I had been in outer space, and I hadn't drifted away for all of eternity. Well, Sox almost had, but I'd saved him. In outer space. *Me.* Izzy Hawthorne, a lifelong astrophobe.

I was gladder than glad to be separated from outer space, but a tiny piece of me had gotten a thrill from it all. Then those feelings went away as I realized the door to the bridge—and to Buzz—had no latch or controls.

"There's no way in!" I groaned.

"Perhaps I could help," Sox said, opening his jaws. He hacked and hacked loudly like he was coughing up a hair ball until a flame shot from his mouth like a blowtorch. I picked him up and cut out an Izzy-sized shape in the door.

As the air lock cutout began to fall, I held on to

Sox and hit my stealth mode button, activating a bubble of invisibility around us. The metal cutout fell with a loud clanky thud. I froze like a statue as both Buzz and the robot jerked their attention right to where I stood.

My heart hammered as I saw how much of the ship's bridge, its command center, looked like a battlefield. The captain's control panel was dented from Buzz's being thrown against it earlier. Smoke clouded the air. Ruined sparking equipment, damaged machine parts, and scorch marks left by fired blasters were everywhere.

A stopped countdown with ten seconds left to go was on a screen.

It was my mistake that had caused all of this, but now it was time for me to fix the mess I'd made.

Buzz tried to grab his wrist blaster, but the robot whipped back around, extending its hand toward him just like it had at the fire geysers. As my stealth mode ran out, I tucked Sox under my arm, raced to Buzz's wrist blaster, and scooped it up.

Buzz got snatched by the extend-o-hand, and he gasped.

Turning to him, I yelled his name.

"Now!" he commanded, his voice strained from his getting squeezed in the robot's grip. Chucking his wrist blaster at him, I held my breath, not wanting a repeat of the last time I'd thrown something to him.

Buzz caught his wrist blaster and fired a laser bolt to sever the long, thick cable of the robot's extend-o-hand. It plunged to the floor, its fingers uncoiling. I felt a flood of relief watching Buzz being set free from those clutches.

And nothing satisfied me more than seeing the robot step back with one fewer hand and tumble over the console with a loud shout.

Sox, Buzz, and I broke into a sprint toward another corridor.

"Come on! Let's get out of here!" Buzz shouted.

Remembering the self-destruct countdown, I shook my head and pointed at the console the robot had fallen behind.

"We have to blow up the ship!" I told him.

It was the only way we could finish this mission once and for all. Otherwise, the robot and its army of zyclopes would retaliate twofold on T'Kani Prime, and all the havoc they'd wreaked before would look like child's play.

Buzz frowned. "There's no time! We'll never make it!"

I pulled the magnetic transport disk off my back and smiled at him.

"Oh, yes, we will," I promised.

As the robot sat up with a grunt, Buzz slipped on his arm blaster, took aim at the self-destruct button, and fired, destroying it completely.

"Self-destruct sequence complete in ten . . ." the ship's operating system announced.

The robot frantically tried to turn off the count-down sequence. Buzz hugged me tight and Sox jumped into his arms as I pressed the button on the transport disk.

Good riddance!

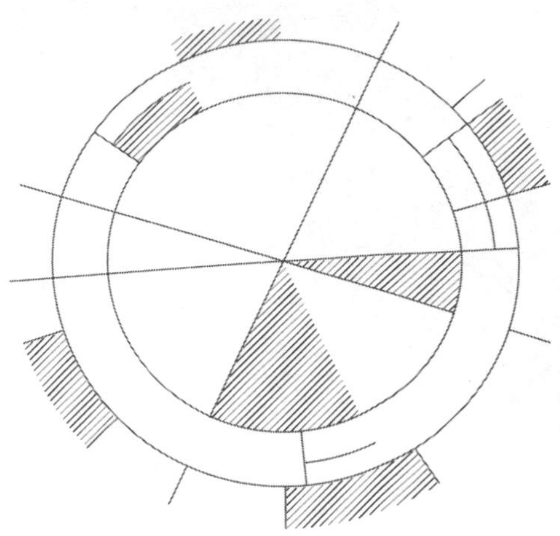

Chapter 21

We blinked out of the bridge and reappeared on the platform in the teleportation bay, standing on top of the Armadillo. Sox, Buzz, and I slid down our ship as Mo and Darby ran back into the teleportation bay. Happiness radiated through me at seeing those two return safely.

"*. . . four . . .*" the countdown continued.

"Let's go!" Buzz panted.

"*. . . three . . .*"

"Everyone, get in before this whole ship explodes!" he commanded.

"*. . . two . . .*"

Everyone except Buzz hurried into the Armadillo. He activated his helmet and raced to the fuel panel. Just as he was about to put in the crystal and its canister, the self-destruct countdown finished.

Oh, no.

My heart stopped beating.

". . . one . . ."

An explosion jostled the whole Zurg ship, making it tilt to its side.

My scream tangled with everyone else's as the Armadillo rolled like a ball off the teleportation platform and down the transport bay. In fact, everything rolled and spilled into the transport bay: Buzz, the robots, and even Buzz's ship, the XL-15.

We tumbled around inside the Armadillo, banging our limbs and heads.

Then a second explosion rattled everything even more, pushing the Armadillo out the bay doors and hurtling us uncontrollably toward T'Kani Prime. The pilot's chair was empty, because Buzz was supposed to fly us out of here, and our power source was gone.

Buzz still had the hyperspeed crystal in his hands.

Through the windows of the Armadillo, we watched Buzz free-fall through the emptiness of space alongside his XL-15. He reached for it but missed, spinning in a wild cartwheel.

As everyone else screamed, I gripped my armrests and said encouragingly through gritted teeth, "Come on, Buzz! Come on. I believe in you!"

He reached for it again, grabbing its wing. Pulling his body closer to the ship, he inserted the hyperspeed crystal and climbed inside the cockpit. Rocket flames shot out of the XL-15 as Buzz started it up and steered it to face us and the Armadillo.

Then another awful explosion swallowed the Zurg ship whole, fiery debris streaking out in all directions. Its force made the Armadillo judder hard and yanked the XL-15 sideways.

I gasped as something emerged from the exploding Zurg ship like a shooting comet of pure vengeance. It was the purple robot!

"No!" I screamed at the top of my lungs. How could that robot have survived all those explosions?

Needing to warn Buzz, I jabbed at my wrist communicator desperately.

"Buzz? Buzz! Can you hear me?" I shouted, but only glitchy static answered me. Worriedly, I looked down at the device, realizing it must've gotten damaged when we rolled around in the spinning Armadillo like garments in a dryer.

"Always be prepared for a challenge!" I reminded myself as a new idea came to me. "Sox, can you transmit to his ship's intercom system?" I asked, anxious.

The Armadillo hurtled through space, and Sox's paws slipped and slid as he tried to keep his balance while his ears spun.

He chanted, "Meow, meow, meow, meow, meow."

As Buzz throttled his engines, trying to right his ship again, the robot latched on to the XL-15, tearing off parts of the ship as if it were made of paper.

Sox's eyelids lowered sadly. "I detected a signal, but I lost it."

I gritted my teeth in anger. The robot's attacks on the XL-15 must have destroyed the signal.

The robot climbed to the fuel cell port, ripped off the panel door, and retrieved the hyperspeed crystal and its canister.

I felt a punch of shock as I finally realized the robot had only ever wanted Buzz's crystal. Was that why the robot and its zyclops army had invaded T'Kani Prime? Because they were waiting for Buzz?

I shook that thought from my head, watching as Buzz ejected from the cockpit of the XL-15, strapped into a jet pack.

The wings of his old Space Ranger suit sprang free and his jet pack generated a powerful blast. Aiming his arm blaster, he shot the crystal. It exploded radiantly, engulfing the robot in the blast.

Sucking in a breath, I widened my eyes in surprise. For decades, he had spent mission after mission in space, trying to stabilize that fuel crystal. Grandma had died believing in him and that crystal.

Now it was gone.

He had sacrificed it to protect all of us.

Buzz flew toward the Armadillo, wrestling to control his flight.

Immediately, I struggled to get to the pilot seat and buckled in, then pulled on the console yoke to try to steer.

"We've entered the planet's gravitational pull. There's no getting out of it without engines," Sox informed me.

"So after all that, we're just gonna crash?" Mo exclaimed.

"I'm afraid so," Sox said sadly.

Suddenly, Buzz flew toward the front of the ship.

"Buzz!" I shouted as he pressed his body against the nose of the Armadillo, trying to use the power of his jet pack to slow down our fall. But it didn't work. Buzz looked behind him as T'Kani Prime grew closer and closer. He pressed against the ship as hard as he could, his jet pack at full blast.

The Armadillo's metallic nose groaned as it cratered from the force.

Buzz stopped, staring at us from the windshield.

My heart stopped, too. Was this it? Was there nothing that could be done?

"I—I can't do it," Buzz said over the radio. As the quaky Armadillo hurtled back toward our home planet, a deep sadness came over me. When the end was near, your panicked brain couldn't help recalling your beginnings. My most important Little Izzy memories rocketed into my head. Grandma was my copilot in each one.

She had always believed in me, just like she had Buzz.

And I had believed in her three rules, following them to a T.

Rule #1: Never stop believing in yourself.

Rule #2: Always believe in the best of people, even if they don't believe in themselves.

Rule #3: Always be prepared for a challenge.

Or at least I thought I had. Turns out I had only pretended to follow Rule #1.

Never stop believing in yourself, Izzy.

I'd studied flight manuals from cover to cover and trained in flight stimulators, but I hadn't believed I was good enough to pilot the Armadillo. I'd fought bugs and wrestled with vines, but I hadn't believed I was brave enough to face outer space.

Grandma's rule sounded easy, but believing in yourself was one of the hardest and scariest things to do.

We had all probably broken Rule #1, but I'd found that if you followed Rule #2, you could learn to see the best in yourself, too. It was okay to do the rules out of order.

"That's okay," I told Buzz.

Buzz nodded at my words, looking straight at me.

"*We* can," I assured him.

His sad expression turned hopeful.

"Can you keep the ship steady?" I asked him.

Buzz nodded, sliding underneath the Armadillo.

"Sox, use your emergency battery to power up the flight controls," I commanded.

Sox obeyed, sticking his tail into the dash. Immediately, the controls lit up, bright and blinking.

"I'll need a copilot," I said. While I sat in the pilot seat, Mo bravely climbed into the cockpit and took over the copilot seat.

I looked at him, instructing him calmly. "Just like the simulator. We pull back on the yoke . . . but nice and easy," I added gently as Mo pulled his yoke hard, making a flap of the Armadillo rip off.

With the Armadillo so close to entering the planet's atmosphere, there was no time to panic or do breathing exercises. Now was the time to prove that I was worthy of being a Space Ranger, and that I was worthy of the Hawthorne family name.

"Yep, sorry. Nice and easy from here in," Mo promised. The Armadillo began to glow with heat as we reentered the atmosphere.

"Okay. Here we go!" Buzz announced as the ship wobbled wildly and plummeted. We squinted as daylight smacked us right in the face.

"We're still coming in too fast!" I shouted, looking around.

Spotting an air brake under a cover on the floor, I instructed, "Darby! The air brake."

Darby bent down and hit the button to open the metal cover, but it only opened slightly.

"It's stuck!" Darby shouted.

"What?" Buzz asked.

"The cover! It's stuck! I need a screwdriver . . . or a hair clip . . . or some sort of small wedge," Darby said.

Mo's eyes grew wide like he'd remembered something important.

"The pen!" he exclaimed. Mo popped it out of his suit and held it up like it was the key to solving our very big problem. Leaning over, he used the pen to pry open the cover.

Darby grunted as she pulled the brake with all her might.

Wind roared around the Armadillo and ripped away more pieces of it as we continued to plunge fast. I held on to the yoke for dear life as the ground came nearer and nearer.

Buzz let go of the Armadillo and flew from underneath it as we landed roughly in the mud-lands outside of the base. We skidded to a hard stop, mud splattering all over the ship.

I couldn't believe it.

We'd done it!

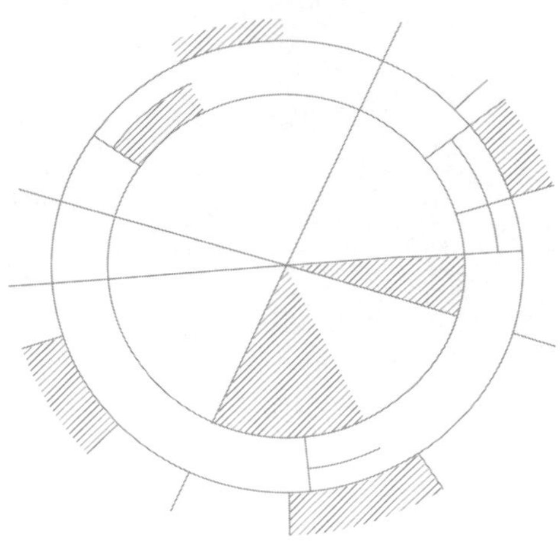

Chapter 22

My body shook with excitement as I sat in the pilot's chair, still gripping the yoke tight. My mouth hung open in shock. We weren't in space or in flames. Happy sunlight from Alpha T'Kani shined through the windshield. Though we hadn't been away for long, I had never been so glad to see the puddly mudlands, the rich green forests, and the Star Command base again.

We'd made it back alive and safe *from outer space* after getting rid of the purple robot and its army of zyclopes once and for all. But none of it would've been possible without resourcefulness, bravery, trust, perseverance, and friendship.

Buzz performed a cool loop in the air and landed perfectly next to the Armadillo. The team and I rushed out of our seats. Mo opened the Armadillo's doors and we poured out, mud squishing under our boots. We surrounded Buzz like a swarm of excited bugs and sandwiched him into a group hug.

"Buzz!" I shouted happily, my arms squeezing tighter.

"Is everyone okay?" he asked, concerned.

"Yeah," Mo and Darby answered.

"I think so," I said.

With the Zurg ship destroyed, the immobilized robots lay lifelessly around the walls of the base, which meant Operation Surprise Party (or Operation Puppet Master, depending on who you asked) had worked!

The sound of incoming sirens startled Darby, and she broke away from the group hug.

"The cops! Everyone, run!" she yelled, fully prepared to flee the scene. Buzz pointed to the fire and rescue trucks making their way to us from the base.

"Wait . . . it's the rescue team," he assured her.

Darby exhaled in relief, her shoulders sagging. "Oh, right. Okay."

"You seem like a decent citizen. What led to your incarceration?" Buzz asked.

"I stole a ship," Darby admitted, shrugging.

Buzz looked at her blankly. "Well, who among us hasn't . . . stolen a ship in a moment of . . . relative desperation?"

I bit back a laugh at his confession.

Buzz had more in common with Darby than he realized.

"I am a man of resources! My weapon is ingenuity!" Mo exclaimed proudly, holding up his handy pen in triumph. "I can do anything!"

"Can you not shout in my ear?" Darby complained grumpily, covering her ears with a wince.

"Ooh, yep. Sorry," Mo apologized with a sheepish smile, dropping his arms.

I gazed up at the blue sky with white fluffy clouds and smiled contentedly. We had destroyed the Zurg ship and turned off the power to all the robots. Everyone on the base was safe. We had made it back to T'Kani Prime alive, but most of all—

"You okay?" Buzz asked, walking up to me.

I pointed up at the sky.

"I was in space," I said. And even though I'd been afraid, I had kept going. Grandma's words came back to me: *That's why it's important to never give up, Izzy, no matter how hard or impossible something seems. Keep trying even if you're afraid. That's bravery.*

I had been in space, and I had been brave.

Buzz nodded with a smile. "Your grandma would be proud."

"She'd be proud of you, too," I said. "She always was."

Pretending I hadn't seen the sacrifice he'd made for us up in space, I asked, "Wait, where's your crystal?"

"It's gone," he admitted, but he didn't seem sad.

"But your mission . . ." I trailed off.

"My mission's been replaced," he said, looking back at the rest of the team, "with something a lot better."

I smiled at that.

Once the vehicles from the base arrived, a troop of Zap Patrol members swarmed us.

"Stop right there!" they ordered, parting to form a path for Commander Burnside. With a stern face, he walked straight up to Buzz.

Uh-oh. He did *not* look happy.

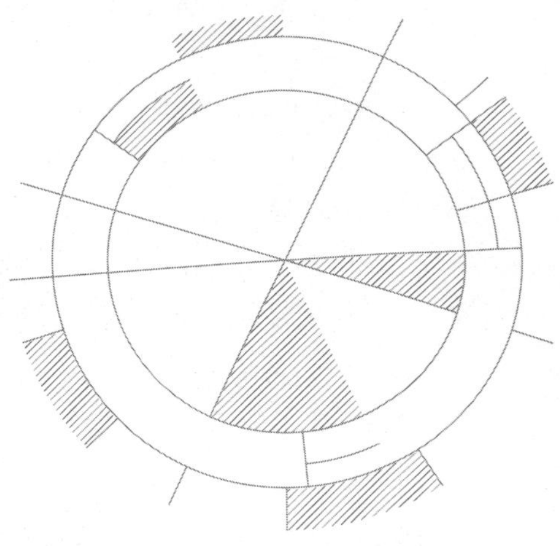

Chapter 23

As Buzz saluted Commander Burnside, the commander's face grew sterner.

"Lightyear," Burnside began, his deep voice full of authority, "you absconded with Star Command property, stole an experimental aircraft, and defied a direct order from your commander. I ought to throw you in the stockade."

Buzz hung his head, admonished.

Worry knotted my insides.

Even though Buzz had committed serious offenses, he had only done it because he didn't want to break his promise to Grandma. After the *Turnip* crash-landed on T'Kani Prime, Buzz had lost his home, time, and friendships. If Commander

Burnside threw him in the stockade, he'd lose his freedom, too.

And if that happened, the team and I would visit him every day, because friends didn't abandon friends in times of need.

"But," Burnside added, "I have other plans for you."

He gestured to the army of fallen robots surrounding the base's towering walls. "These robots were no match for our laser shield. But we may not be so fortunate the next time. That's where you come in. We want you to start a new version of the Space Ranger Corps: Universe Protection Division."

Then Burnside's hard face softened as he looked at Buzz, sincere.

"You're going to be a Space Ranger again, Buzz."

At the news, Buzz's face fell in shock.

Burnside pointed to the surrounding security soldiers. "You can hand-select your team from the very best of our Zap Patrol and train them to your liking."

The Zap Patrol lowered their weapons and saluted Buzz.

"Hup-hup!" they chorused.

They even *hup-hup*ed better than us.

Buzz looked at the Zap Patrol and smiled, but his smile faded away quickly.

He turned back to Commander Burnside. "Well, that's very kind of you, sir. But . . . I'm afraid I'm going to have to decline."

Surprised, I felt my jaw go slack. All Buzz had wanted was to be an *official* Space Ranger again! He wouldn't have to steal ships or do solo missions anymore. He'd have a fancy new ship and an elite crew. Why would he say no to Commander Burnside's offer?

"I already have my team," Buzz said, looking back at me, Darby, Mo, and Sox.

I stared back at him in disbelief, my brain attempting to compute his words. Buzz Lightyear, the last Space Ranger, had chosen a ragtag crew of cadets (and a robotic feline companion) over the ultra-elite Zap Patrol?

Yeah, we had just saved T'Kani Prime together, but—

No, wait. No ifs, ands, or buts.

We had saved T'Kani Prime!

If we could do that, *we* were the very best of the best.

With a nod, I smiled. "You sure do."

The rescue team drove us all back to the base. A big crowd gathered outside of Star Command Headquarters, cheering for us. Wow! When you saved an entire planet from doom and destruction, word traveled fast. We waved, smiled, and accepted high fives as we walked through the crowd to go inside. A group of security guards escorted us, with Commander Burnside and Buzz at the helm.

In the headquarters lobby, there was a portrait of Grandma in her commander uniform. It was the only picture of her on *all* of T'Kani Prime where she didn't smile, but her face shined with Hawthorne pride.

I stopped in front of it and thought about Grandma's three rules and how much they had helped me.

Rule #1: Never stop believing in yourself.

I might have been a Hawthorne, but being Izzy was just as important.

Rule #2: Always believe in the best of people, even if they don't believe in themselves.

Believing in each other was the most powerful weapon. It was what had destroyed the robot and its Zurg ship.

Rule #3: Always be prepared for a challenge.

I had journeyed into space and conquered my fears.

I, Izzy Hawthorne, was brave.

"I hope I made you proud, Grandma," I whispered. My imagination brought the portrait to life. I imagined her warm smile and kind eyes aimed at me. I pictured her reaching out to me and cupping my cheek tenderly.

I always believed in you, Izzy, I thought she'd say.

A security guard cleared her throat and my imagination faded away. Grandma was a picture again, but I had her Space Ranger suit, her words of wisdom, and my memories of her. Those would never fade away.

"This way, please," the guard said to me. We caught up with the rest of the group. When Mo's stomach growled, he smiled sheepishly.

Commander Burnside pointed to a break room filled with vending machines. "After a mission like yours, our new Universe Protection Division will need to engage in a Star Command Code 28-0-6.2 to refuel your strength. You'll need every bit of it."

A few hours earlier, we had just been the Junior Patrol, hiding out at the outpost while zyclopes stomped around. Now, after saving our home, we'd been promoted to Space Rangers. I'd studied, trained, and waited my entire life for this, but I had to admit it was a little weird hearing Commander Burnside call us something other than cadets.

We all went in, but Commander Burnside told Buzz to stop.

"Not you, Lightyear," he said, walking on. "You'll come with me."

"Yes, sir," Buzz said with a nod, then looked back at us. "Commander Burnside will be expecting a debrief of our mission."

I nodded at Buzz, watching him leave. It felt like we could *all* use a break and debrief.

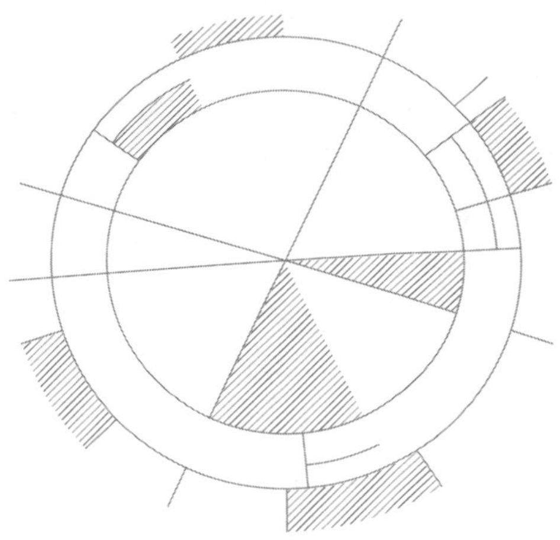

Chapter 24

Mo went to a vending machine and got us sandwiches. He passed one to Darby and tried to give one to me, but I shook my head and said, "No, thanks." You'd think being chased by robots, tiptoeing around bugs, walking through space, rescuing Buzz from the robot, and piloting the Armadillo would have given me a mighty appetite, but I didn't have one.

I was hungry for another adventure, not food!

Mo offered my sandwich to Sox.

"Thank you, but I'm a robot," Sox reminded Mo before hopping into my lap. "A petting would be nice, though."

"You've more than earned one, Sox." I smiled, rubbing his fuzzy orange head. He purred loudly.

Mo laughed. "Oops, forgot about the you're-a-talking-robot-cat part. More for me."

He plopped onto a couch, propped up his muddy boots, and ripped open his first snack's packaging, then hummed contentedly as he took a big juicy bite.

"If you don't get your dirty boots off that couch, Burnside will put *you* on parole," Darby warned jokingly.

He stopped chewing and took his boots off the couch. He used his elbow to try to buff out the mud stain, but it only made the smudge worse. Darby sat back and laughed, but Mo didn't mind it; he started to laugh, too.

"We rescued an entire planet. I think that trumps a little mud," Mo said, pumping his sandwich triumphantly in the air.

"You're right. If we're the Universe Protection Division now, that means Burnside will scrub my criminal file clean," Darby said, chewing thoughtfully.

Mo grinned, saying, "Yeah, you're right. We do make a good team."

They gave each other juicy fist bumps.

I smiled at them, happy to see them getting along once and for all. I guessed nearly dying together had brought them closer. Sometimes it took nearly losing someone to make you appreciate them more.

I asked them about their mission on the Zurg ship.

"Oh, boy. Where do we begin?" Darby said while chewing. "After you and the cat left, this one grabbed a transport disk and dropped it on its button, so it kept falling on the teleportation platform in a loop." She jerked a wet thumb at Mo.

I covered my mouth and laughed, picturing it all in my head.

Sox chuckled, too. "That must've been a sight."

"Hey, it was a mistake!" Mo defended himself.

"Then we had to figure out a way to close the door to the teleportation bay," Darby continued, "and I found the button—"

Mo interrupted, "But when she pressed it, the doors closed and she triggered the alarm."

Sox and I looked at each other in shock.

"That would explain why we got locked inside that room of windows," Sox said.

My brain teleported me back to that moment. I remembered how afraid I was, being trapped in a room where *only glass* separated me from the inky blackness of space. But it had taken floating through it in Grandma's Space Ranger suit and hurtling across it in the Armadillo to realize there was something much worse than astrophobia.

Like losing a friend.

"Okay, I might've triggered the security system and had the robots coming after us, but I had a plan B," Darby said matter-of-factly, holding up a finger.

I sat on the edge of my seat, excited to hear more. "What did you do?"

"I used a transport disk, a gum wrapper, and some chewed-up gum to make a bomb to blow up some robots," Darby answered around her sandwich.

I crinkled my nose. "Where did you get the chewed-up gum?"

"From me. It was a yummy raspberry flavor, too," Mo said, then asked Darby if she had any more.

Darby shook her head, chewing. "Nope, that was my last piece."

"Aw," Mo whined, disappointedly taking a bite of his sandwich.

"To activate the bomb, a robot had to step on it, but in case they didn't, we had to use something heavy," Darby said. Then they both took turns telling the rest of the story, which involved unscrewing screws, dropping a cooling unit onto the bomb, and using Darby's surrender string to roll away after the bomb's explosion.

"Whoa," I said, clapping my hands. "Bravo!"

"Now it's your turn," Mo urged.

I gazed up at the ceiling, imagining it was all blackness and burning stars.

"We were in space," I said, smiling. I told them about my space walk with Sox and how terribly afraid I had been at first.

"Up there, I almost drifted away, and Izzy saved me," Sox said, snuggling his head against my hand.

I petted him, smiling as he purred loudly. "I'd do all of it over again, too."

Wanting to help Buzz in his battle against the robot had motivated me to do things I had thought were too scary and impossible.

"You did a pretty good job up there yourself,

kid," Darby said to me. "It isn't easy conquering your fears. We're all proud of you. Your grandma would be proud of you, too."

I looked at each of them. "Grandma would be proud of you guys, too. We all make amazing Space Rangers."

Earlier in the day, we had been the Junior Patrol. Now we were Space Rangers of the Universe Protection Squad. Achieving your dreams was a nice way to end a nightmarish day like this one.

Mo looked down at his Space Ranger suit, which was covered in meat juice. "Yeah, being one is pretty cool. Do you think we'll get cooler suits and cooler pens?"

"Of course!" I assured him. "New division, new suits!"

I loved wearing Grandma's suit. It had served me well on this mission, but it was time to put it away and get one of my own.

"Imagine *all* the explosions we can make with new weapons they'll give us," Darby sighed dreamily.

"Imagine *all* the adventures we'll go on," I said.

When it was Sox's turn to speak, he stayed quiet. At first I figured maybe robotic cats didn't have wants and dreams, but then I realized something was distracting him.

"What's wrong, Sox?"

"I'm compiling an internal report of Operation Surprise Party Puppet Master, cataloging all the events that transpired for Buzz's mission log," Sox said. When he mentioned the words *puppet master*, Mo grinned from ear to ear. I fought the urge to roll my eyes.

"However, my memory recalls the double signal on the enemy's ship that led us in the false direction. I cannot compute a logical explanation for it," Sox went on, his tone curious. I remembered how confused Sox had been by the mysterious double signal.

"I guess we'll never know now," I said.

"Not knowing is the worrying part, Izzy," Sox sighed.

I petted his head to give him some comfort. Maybe robotic cats did have wants, dreams, fears, and worries like humans. Since Grandma had played a part in designing him to be a good friend to Buzz, it made sense that he wasn't an emotionless robot like the zyclopes.

I opened my mouth to reassure him that

everything would be okay, but the door to the break room opened and Buzz came inside. His gaze landed on each of us, one at a time. His face was blank and unreadable. Worry lumped up in my throat as I thought the worst. After his debrief with Commander Burnside, had he changed his mind about wanting us as his team?

Ready to remind him why we deserved to be the Universe Protection Division, I started, "B—"

"Are you ready for our next mission, team?" he asked, his face lighting up with a smile.

IZZY AND GRANDMA'S BLAST FROM THE PAST

Grandma's Old Missions

Sometimes after school me and Dad played one of his video games. One day, we were playing one where our avatars had to return a magical gem to its temple, but vicious plant monsters in the jungles wanted it for themselves. So we had to use laser swords to battle them. Dad's forehead wrinkled when he concentrated on playing his video games. His fingers hit the colorful buttons and used the joysticks on his game controller lightning fast. Grandma Kiko liked games, and she'd taught Dad how to play when he was little. Then he taught me how to play, too.

Back then, we'd played all the games on Easy Mode, but now we played on Expert Mode, which was the hardest to beat.

A, A, B, A. Up, down, up, down, left, left, right. I pressed those buttons quickly so my avatar could slash at a gigantic tree monster blocking the ancient temple.

"Ya, ya, hmm, ya," my avatar said.

"Ha-ha, grr, grr," Dad's avatar said, slicing off the tree's limbs. After we won the fight, our avatars rushed into the temple and returned the gem to its original spot.

"Mission complete," the game announced. Me and Dad grinned at each other and high-fived.

"We make a great team, sweetheart!" Dad exclaimed.

"Yeah, we do!" I agreed, clasping my hands together. "Can we *please* play another round?"

Dad looked at the time on his watch, shaking his head. "It's time for you to go see your grandma. She could use some cheering up."

"Roger that," I said, hopping to my feet. I gave Dad a salute, then left our apartment to go see Grandma. The walk to the hospital building wasn't very far. When I got to her room, the door opened for me.

Grandma sat on her bed, staring at her tablet with a smile.

"Hi, Grandma!" I greeted her, running into her room.

She looked up and smiled at me. "Hi, sweetheart. Come join me."

I climbed onto her hospital bed and settled beside her.

"What are you up to, Grandma?" I asked, leaning over to see what was on her tablet that made her smile.

"Just looking through my old field journal," she said, pointing to a sketch of an orange octopus-like three-beaked alien and the report she'd written about meeting it.

"It's a native species to a planet light-years away from here," Grandma explained. "They live in trees and build nests like birds. They're very friendly. Buzz didn't like them very much."

"Why didn't he like it, Grandma?" I asked.

"Because one accidentally fell from a tree and landed on his head," she said, laughing at the memory. "Luckily, he was wearing his helmet, but its tentacles were slimy like snot. He couldn't wipe the stuff off his helmet."

She used her finger to swipe to the next page of her field journal, where there was a picture of her friend Buzz wearing a slime-covered helmet. She laughed harder, and I giggled, too. I learned about scaly cave-dwelling creatures, ten-legged doglike beings, and lots more. She had pictures of red jungles, underground caverns with purple water, and snowy green mountains from the planets she'd visited all across the universe.

Grandma had so many stories about her Space Ranger adventures with her friend Buzz Lightyear. Together, they had outrun rivers of lava from erupting volcanos and ridden on the backs of gigantic bird aliens like cowboys.

After all her storytelling, she put aside her tablet and sighed tiredly.

"Those days are behind me now," she said, reminiscing.

"Do you miss it, Grandma?" I asked.

"Of course, sweetheart. I miss being out among the stars. I miss all the adventures, but more than anything, I miss my friend Buzz," she said.

I snuggled up to her and said, "I want to go on adventures just like you and Buzz Lightyear."

She smiled at me, resting her cheek on my head. "Oh, you will, Izzy. You'll have lots and lots of adventures as a Space Ranger. You might even have some with Buzz."

"How, Grandma? Isn't he an old man?"

She laughed, shaking her head. "No, sweetheart. I'm the only one getting old. It's hard to explain now, but I think you two would make very good partners."

When I had visited her the day before, there was only one framed photo on the small table by her hospital bed. She had asked Dad to bring that family photo to keep her company. But today there was another photo.

She picked it up gently and showed it to me.

I knew it was an old picture, because Grandma looked much younger in her gray commander uniform, and Buzz stood right beside her in his training sweatsuit. Both smiled for the camera, but Grandma's smile was a proud one.

"When he comes back in a year or two, he won't look much different than he does in this photo," Grandma said, pointing to him. "He's gonna take you all back home in the *Turnip*."

Grandma talked like she would be left behind on T'Kani Prime.

"But what about you, Grandma?" I asked, frowning.

She smiled sadly. "Don't worry about me, sweetheart. I'll always be with you, no matter what you do or where you go. Because I'll be in here and in here." She gave my chest and my head each a little poke. Then she tickled my tummy a little, making me squirm and laugh.

When she yawned, I yawned, too.

My eyes grew heavy as I got really tired.

"You have so many adventures ahead of you, Izzy," Grandma whispered to me as I fell asleep beside her.

In my dreams, all of my adventures were with her.

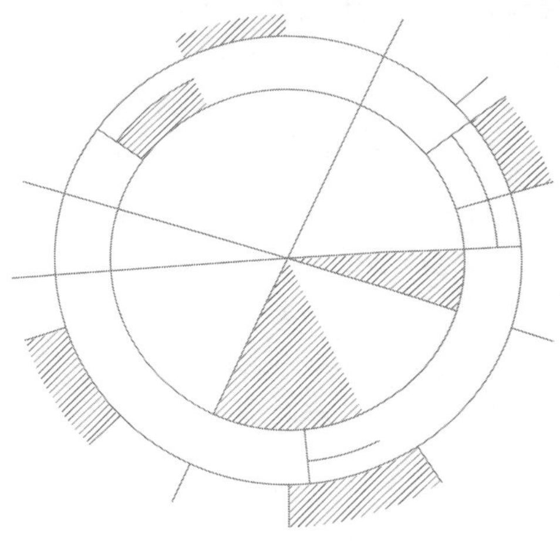

Chapter 25

A few months later . . .

It was Launch Day. The five of us walked down a corridor in the new Space Ranger suits Commander Burnside had commissioned for us.

During Buzz's debrief with Burnside, he'd learned that the Star Command leaders had found suspicious readings in a nearby quadrant. Buzz had been tasked with starting a new version of the Space Ranger Corps: Universe Protection Division, and he'd chosen *us* to join his elite squad.

We were his team. And now we were Space Rangers—*together.*

"These new suits are amazing. Arm blaster,

rocket wings," I said excitedly. "Man, I would have loved some rocket wings out there in space."

Mo examined his suit, disappointed. "Could use a pen, though."

"Pens are for rookies. You're not a rookie," Buzz reminded him.

Darby held up her arm blaster, grinning cheekily. "I can't believe I'm allowed to carry this."

Then she looked at her other arm. "I wish I had two of them."

"You got a clean record and you're free and armed. How are you still complaining?" Mo asked, shaking his head slowly.

"I got off on good behavior," Darby reminded him with a shrug, "not good attitude."

As Sox strolled alongside us in a half suit, he said, "You know, I never wear pants, but suddenly it feels weird not wearing pants. Does it look weird without pants?"

"Nah, you look good," Mo assured him, giving the robotic cat a thumbs-up.

"I can't wait to get out of here and engage in a Star Command Code 28-0-6.2," I said giddily, excited about our first official mission.

Buzz turned to me, raising his eyebrows. "You mean a snack break?"

I blinked, confused. "What?"

"'Cause you just gave the code for a snack break," Buzz said, pointing at me.

"No, I didn't," I insisted, shaking my head.

"Uh, did I just hear the code for nutritional intake? Should we delay the launch?" asked someone from the intercom system above our heads. You'd think after years of studying Grandma's Academy manuals, I'd know the difference between Star Command Code 28-0-6.2 and Star Command Code 28-0-6.3.

Again, I shook my head, smiling. "No, we're fine. Sorry. Thank you."

Though a meat-bread-meat sandwich did sound good.

"Hey. Happens to the best of us," Buzz said, putting his hand on my shoulder.

We passed a statue of Grandma in her commander uniform, and the sight of it filled me with warmth. She always knew I'd be a Space Ranger one day, blasting off into space with Buzz at my side. She had seen the best in me long before I ever did.

Now, in a way, she was with me, cheering me on. Not just as a statue, but as memories.

You'd make an excellent Space Ranger.

I did, Grandma. I did.

We entered the enormous launch bay. Our boots crossed over a large emblem of the Space Ranger Corps on the concrete floor. Bright lights from the ceilings beamed down on us, making our new suits glint. Ahead of us, our new ship glistened, too.

In Space Ranger tradition, Buzz grazed his fingers against the ship's shiny hull, and we all followed suit. Once inside, he settled into the cockpit as our pilot. As copilot, I sat beside him. Excitedly, I looked at an extensive console of screens, buttons, switches, and levers, knowing the name and function for each one.

Mo and Darby seated themselves behind us. A patient Sox remained on the floor by our feet, waiting for Buzz's command.

Commander Burnside's voice came through the cockpit's intercom system: *"All right, team. As members of the elite Universe Protection Unit of the Space Ranger Corps, you'll protect the galaxy from the threat of invasion from any sworn enemies of the Galactic Alliance."*

Even though the robots and the Zurg ship were no longer a threat to us, we were far from safe from danger.

As pilot and copilot, Buzz and I did our pre-launch check, flipping switches, pressing buttons, and pulling levers. Our ship rolled slowly to the launch silo, then latched on to the launch tower and rose vertically into a launch position

Moments away from blastoff, I breathed in deeply and exhaled to calm myself down as excitement bubbled inside of me.

Buzz picked up a rectangular cartridge and inserted it into the control console.

"Hello. I am your Internal Voice-Activated Navigator," IVAN greeted us in a friendly voice.

"Good to have you back, IVAN," Buzz said, sounding pleased.

"Captain Lightyear, ready for launch," a controller reported through the intercom.

Buzz smiled at all of us, then looked up to the sky at the end of the silo's vertical tunnel. In a few moments, we'd blast into it, through it, and beyond. I looked at him as his face went blank and he became lost in thought.

"Buzz?" I asked.

"Huh?" He blinked as if he'd forgotten where he was and who he was with.

"You okay?"

My question made him smile at me, and once again he looked like the same old Buzz.

"I am now," he assured me. I smiled back, confident we were ready to take on whatever came next.

Sox leapt up from the floor, flipped open the tip of his tail, and inserted the connector into the dashboard to power the control panel. The cockpit shook harder and harder as the ship prepared for takeoff.

"All right, Space Rangers. Here we go," Buzz said.

And that was when it hit me: After all those years of dreaming and training, this was really real. I was a Space Ranger.

But more importantly, I had found my own way of being a Space Ranger. I had overcome my fear and done things my way—the only way I could.

I held my finger out to Buzz, and he tapped against it with his own. Together, we pulled back our hands and made an explosion sound.

"To infinity . . ." I started.

"And beyond," Buzz finished.

Get ready, universe. Space Ranger Izzy Hawthorne is on her way.